W251r

ROXANNE BOOKMAN: LIVE AT FIVE!

by Cathy Warren

BRADBURY PRESS   NEW YORK

Bradbury Press
An Affiliate of Macmillan, Inc.
866 Third Avenue, New York, N.Y. 10022
Collier Macmillan Canada, Inc.
Printed and bound in the United States of America
10   9   8   7   6   5   4   3   2   1

The text of this book is set in 10.5 pt. ITC Bookman Light.

LIBRARY OF CONGRESS CATALOGING-IN-PUBLICATION DATA
Warren, Cathy.
Roxanne Bookman: live at five! / by Cathy Warren.
p.   cm.
Summary: Feeling like a loser compared to the other talented
members of her family, ten-year-old Roxanne hopes to find success
competing with her class in a television quiz show.
ISBN 0-02-792492-0
[1. Winning and losing—Fiction. 2. Schools—Fiction.
3. Contests—Fiction.]   I. Title.
PZ7.W2514Ro 1988
[Fic]—dc19   88-964   CIP   AC

For my sister, Bobbi,

who taught me how to play ball

ROXANNE BOOKMAN:
LIVE AT FIVE!

"Roxanne, you've hardly touched my famous Saturday Night Bookman Burgers," Dad said, hurt. "Don't you like them anymore?"

"I love them," I said. I picked up my burger and tried to take another bite, but it was no use. I was too nervous to eat.

"I think she has a touch of pregame jitters," Mom said, soothing Dad's feelings.

"Jitters? Why, Roxanne can get a hit off any pitcher in the league," said Dad.

"Not off Claudia Slooder," Trip reminded them. "Roxanne hasn't gotten one hit off Claudia in the last three games against Edgebrook." He grabbed another burger off the platter.

"Thanks, Trip," I said in my best sarcastic voice. Just thinking about Claudia made my stomach do flip-flops. In less than two hours my team, the Lazy Hills Hornets, would be facing Claudia and the Edgebrook Eagles in the baseball battle of the season: the

Pony League Championship. All season Claudia has succeeded in shaking my confidence. She's so sure of herself!

I guess I looked miserable because Dad tried to cheer me up, but what he said next made me feel worse.

"Roxanne! We Bookmans are winners. Don't be timid. Get out there and show them what you're made of. That's how Trip made it onto the varsity football team, isn't it, Trip?"

"Yeah, sure, Dad," Trip said.

"Why, I'm more convinced than ever that you can do anything you put your mind to," Dad said. He pushed his chair back from the table and smiled broadly.

"Well . . . ," said Mom hesitantly.

"You're not having second thoughts about auditioning, are you?" asked Dad.

Trip kicked me under the table. We both knew Dad felt Mom had outgrown her secretarial job at Channel Six. He wanted her to try out as host of a new segment on the "Live at Five" news called "Around Town." Mom thought Suzy Slooder, Claudia's mom, would probably win since she was already a reporter on the show. Still, Dad had talked her into setting up an audition for Monday after work.

"Of course I'm not having second thoughts," said Mom.

"Good, because you practically run that station as it is," Dad said.

2

"Oh, let's not talk about me," Mom said quickly. She stacked up the nearby empty dishes, then she said, "Besides, Bill, you're the one we should be proud of. Kids, your dad's too modest to brag, but his new engineering company just won the contract to design the bridge over in Milwood!"

I congratulated Dad and tried to look cheerful. Great, I thought, just what I needed to hear. It was hard enough being a Bookman when everyone in my family was good at something. Did they have to be practically fearless, too?

"Now, Roxanne, getting back to the point I was trying to make." Dad got this faraway look in his eyes. "I remember back when I was playing baseball, I went into a slump for . . ."

"Bill," Mom said, shaking her head.

"Well, that was a long time ago," he said. "Betsy, do you remember when Trip was in the Pony League play-offs?"

Mom's face clouded over, the way it always does when Dad brings up the subject of Trip and his baseball days. Mom stood up and started clearing the table. I'd give anything to know what happened. But no one will discuss it with me.

"What I meant was, we were all too nervous to eat . . . ," Dad called after her as she carried the plates into the kitchen.

I gathered up some more plates and followed her.

"Shouldn't you be getting ready for the game?" she asked.

"I have plenty of time," I said, grabbing a dish towel. Secretly, I wished that we could just forget about the game. Maybe by the time we remembered, it would be over.

Mom filled the sink with soapy water and started to wash the dishes.

"Mom, am I really a Bookman?" I asked quietly. Then I busied myself drying the spoons and lining them up in a neat stack.

"Why, Roxanne," she said, letting a plate settle back down into the water. "We've gone over this a million times. You know perfectly well that even though you're a redhead and the rest of us all have dark hair and brown eyes, you are a Bookman!"

"It's just that sometimes I don't feel like a Bookman," I cried. "I feel like a ten-year-old loser!"

"You're not a loser," she said. "Anyway, winning isn't everything." She pulled the stopper out of the suds.

"That's easy for you to say. You and Dad and Trip are all winners. I'll bet you've never even been afraid of anything."

"Don't be silly, I'm afraid sometimes," she said. "As for me being a winner, I haven't even auditioned yet. I think you're just nervous about the game. Don't worry, we'll be there, and we'll be proud of you even if you lose."

"Great," I cried, "I want you to be proud of me for winning, not losing!"

"If you feel like a winner, you are a winner," she said resolutely.

"Mom!"

"What?"

"Never mind," I said. "You don't understand."

Trip came up behind me and nudged me out of the way.

"I don't know what you're bellyaching about," he said, opening the cupboard. "You get to have Mr. Duggins for a coach and a fifth-grade teacher. You're the lucky one. You ought to see *our* coach!"

He pulled down a box of crackers.

Mom let out a long sigh and put her hands on her hips.

"Trip Bookman! Don't tell me you're still hungry!"

"Starved," he said.

"For goodness sakes!" she whispered. "After the dinner your father cooked? Don't let him see you, it would hurt his feelings." She turned to me. "Roxanne, you didn't eat much."

"Don't worry, Mom. I'm sure Coach Duggins will take the team to Joe's Burger Barn after the game, even if they *lose*," Trip said, laughing.

"Thanks for the vote of confidence, Trip," I said. Normally, the thought of going to Joe's and having cheeseburgers and malts would have cheered me right up. I love hearing Mr. Duggins tell his *Mad Men from Mars* stories and I love it when he plays Twenty Questions with us. But ever since the play-offs, Mr. Duggins has had a strange gleam in his eyes. All he talks about is winning. That's why, secretly, the kids on our team have started calling him Mad Dog.

"You'd better run ahead, Roxanne," Mom said. "And don't worry, Trip's just teasing you. We'll all be there and we'll be rooting for you."

I grabbed my lucky bat from the hall closet. It's a wooden Louisville Slugger that Trip gave me for my eighth birthday. Then I ran the four blocks from my house to McGiver Field. Even though the sun was setting it was still about a zillion degrees outside. By the time I reached the field, my T-shirt was sticking to my skin.

It was cool and dark inside the dugout. I was relieved to see that my best friend, Abby, was already there. She was sitting between Ronald and Philip. When my eyes had adjusted to the dark, I noticed that she and I were both wearing our red Burger Barn T-shirts, the ones with the pictures of giant cheeseburgers on the front. At least we matched. Everybody else on the team was wearing something different. For the first time all summer I felt kind of embarrassed and wished we had been able to scrape the money together earlier for new uniforms. They still hadn't arrived. Next to the Edgebrook Eagles, we'd probably look like a hand-me-down team.

"Here, Rox, sit on the box," said Ronald. He pointed to a wooden crate on the other side of him.

"She's sitting next to me, so move," said Abby.

I leaned around Abby and made a big deal about saying hello to Philip. He's sort of spaced out and if I don't get his attention right away, it can be hours before he notices me. He's usually daydreaming about Reggie Jackson. He wants to be just like him when he grows up. He's already tall and strong and the best overall player on the team.

Just being with my friends made me feel good. We were the old gang, the only original members of our first-grade class left. I closed my eyes, took a deep breath, and thought about how the four of us had been through a lot together. Once, in the third grade, Mom got free tickets for our class to be in the Channel Six studio for "Mr. Clown's Happy Hour." I was supposed to give the tickets to our teacher, Mrs. Green, but I talked Abby, Ronald, and Philip into helping me sell them instead. We used the money we made to buy hot fudge sundaes. Even though it was all my idea, when Mom caught us, they stood by me. Ever since, they kid me and say I remind them of Lucy in the old "I Love Lucy" shows.

When I opened my eyes and looked up, I noticed that the four new kids who had transferred over from Milwood were coming down into the dugout. Janet and the Pilcher twins, Erwin and George, were the last to arrive.

Janet was rummaging around in the glove bin. She had just unearthed her special left-handed glove when Mad Dog hurried down the steps.

"Hey! We're looking good," he cried. "What are we going to do tonight?"

"Win," Ronald said.

"I can't hear you," Mad Dog called out, cupping his hand over his ear.

"Win!" we all shouted.

"One more time!"

"Win!" we yelled.

"That's better," he said. He was beaming.

I was sure he was going to rush over to the portable chalkboard and start drawing a bunch of stick figures and call out new plays or talk strategy, but he surprised me by saying, "Team, I know you're all excited. So let's just review some of the basics to calm us down." He grabbed a bat and stood in front of us to demonstrate. "All right, as you remember, we talked about batting at the beginning of the season. What steps do we take when we bat?"

"Wait, watch, swing, and follow-through," we said in unison.

"Terrific," he said. He had a wide grin on his face. "Today, the important thing to remember is that baseball is a team sport. Teamwork is essential if we're going to beat Edgebrook. I don't want any superstars. I don't want any *hot dogs* out there. We'll work together. If we win, great! If we don't, it doesn't matter. I want you to know, it won't make any difference to me."

I didn't know who he thought he was fooling. Abby looked at me and rolled her eyes.

"We just have to win for him," she whispered. "We just have to!"

We all wanted Mad Dog to win the Coach of the Year trophy, and not just because he would be our teacher in two days. We wanted him to win because he deserved it. He had taken our ragtag team and taught us how to play ball.

The lights had been turned on and it was finally cooling down. There was a nice balmy breeze, and I could smell the aroma of hot buttered popcorn coming from the bleachers. Since we were the home team, we were in the field first and I hurried to my position at shortstop. Philip sprinted up to the pitcher's mound and started his warm-up. He stretched his long brown arms up over his head, then brought them down to his chest and fired the ball across the plate to Erwin, our catcher.

Before I knew it, the inning was under way and Philip had struck out the first two batters. Then Janet caught a fly for an easy third out and we headed in to the dugout.

I follow Philip in the batting lineup, so I grabbed my bat and hurried to the on-deck circle to warm up. The crowd was cheering wildly. I turned around and saw that Mom and Dad and Trip were clapping. I was feeling pretty confident until the Eagles broke their huddle and swarmed out onto the field. All together, they looked awesome in their bright new uniforms.

They kicked up little clouds of dust and chanted, "Lazy Hills can't bat. Lazy Hills can't bat." Claudia stood on the pitcher's mound, her blond hair tucked up under her baseball cap. She had a smirk on her face. Just looking at her made me want to run away.

Philip tapped the ground three times with his bat. He was raring to go. Claudia took her time. She cupped the ball to her face until we were tired of waiting. Then she wound her arm around several times and pitched the ball across the plate. On the third pitch, Philip hit the ball high and soaring, past their second baseman. He made it to first easily. I picked up my bat and hurried into position. From the bleachers, Mom and Dad yelled, "Let's go, Roxanne!" Then Trip shouted, "Rox, hit it between second and third. They don't have any coverage there!"

What a joke! With Claudia on the mound, I'd be lucky to get a hit, let alone aim one. I ran my hands along the smooth grain of the wood, trying to calm down. My heart was beating so wildly, I was surprised to see that the cheeseburger on my shirt wasn't thumping. When I glanced back at the bleachers, Dad gave me the thumbs-up sign. I took a deep breath and turned toward Claudia.

"Roxanne, you've met your match," Claudia called out to me.

"Oh yeah," I called back. "I can hit anything you can throw."

"We'll see about that." She grinned a phony grin.

Then she turned sideways on the mound and held the ball in front of her. I could see her watching Philip out of the corner of her eye. I was readjusting my grip and planting my feet when she sent the first ball sailing past me.

"Strike one!" cried the umpire.

I couldn't concentrate on the ball. I swung wildly at the next pitch and ticked it.

"Strike two!"

I couldn't let Claudia beat me again. I had to show her once and for all. I had to concentrate. I had to watch the ball. I saw it leave her hand and come screaming across the plate. I swung at it with all my might. But my timing was off.

"Strike three!"

Abby hit a fly ball for our second out. Then George singled and Philip advanced to third. While Erwin was at bat, George stole second base. Then Erwin hit Philip and George in. Claudia walked Janet and then Ronald tapped a slow grounder to first for our last out.

We were a little jumpy in the top of the second inning, and we let Edgebrook get some runs. I missed a fly ball. Then Abby fumbled an easy out at first. After a while, though, we settled down and started working as a team. Whenever a ball came rocketing out between second and third, I dove for it, scooped it up, and fired it to Abby. The Hornets were hot!

Finally it was the bottom of the last inning and the

score was tied, Edgebrook 12, Lazy Hills 12. I was jogging back to the dugout when Claudia bumped into me, blocking my path.

"Is it true that your mother is going to try to compete against mine for that new show?" she demanded.

"Yeah, I guess so," I mumbled.

"Isn't your mother just a plain old secretary at the station?"

"There's nothing plain about my mom," I said hotly.

"We'll see about that." She headed for the pitcher's mound.

By the time it was my turn at bat, the bases were loaded with Janet on third, Ronald on second, and Philip on first. There were two outs. Mad Dog ran up to me as I was leaving the on-deck circle. "So far so good," he said. "Now, I've told the others and I want you to pay attention. I know you can hit, Roxanne, but we want to play it safe. We're going to try to walk Janet in for our winning run. Claudia's tired and her pitches are wild, so I'm sure you won't have any trouble getting a walk. Remember, just stand still and let her do all the work. Whatever you do, don't try to hit a home run or be a superstar. We're going to win this game!"

He ran back to the dugout.

"Remember, Roxanne, teamwork!" he called out.

I looked at Claudia, then back at the bleachers. Trip and Mom and Dad were all cheering for me.

I stepped up to the plate. Beads of perspiration were streaming down my face. I felt everyone's eyes bearing down on me. They were depending on me. My hands were wet and clammy and they stuck in odd positions on the bat. I put it down, wiped my hands on my T-shirt, and got a better grip. My heart was thumping and my ears were ringing. I dug my feet in and stood very still.

"Ball one," cried the umpire.

I stayed rigid and let another one by.

"Ball two."

"Coward!" Claudia yelled.

I blinked my eyes and rolled my shoulders. Claudia threw the third pitch high and to the outside.

"Ball three."

"Cluck, cluck, cluck."

The crowd was hushed. This was it. I squared my shoulders and concentrated on watching the ball as it left Claudia's hand and started coming toward me. I can't really explain what happened next, except to say that all of a sudden, I knew the pitch was mine.

I saw the ball coming toward me in a shaft of silver light. I started swinging. My whole body moved into the ball. I felt the quiver of wood, the ripple of motion as it connected with the ball. Then I heard the cracking sound, firecracker crisp as the ball soared out between first and second. I dropped the bat and started running. I heard the sound of my feet as they pounded the hard ground. I raced past first and on toward second. I felt the warm night air rush against my wet face. My heart was thumping wildly. If I could just make it into home, we would win. The players were a blur as I raced past them. I bumped into something as I rounded third. Screams were coming from the bleachers. I was almost there, almost home.

"Claudia Slooder, eat my dust!" I yelled. I dove toward home plate and slid all the way to the fence.

When I looked up, Claudia was doubled over with laughter. Something was wrong. The scoreboard still read Edgebrook 12, Lazy Hills 12.

"Roxanne! What were you doing?" Abby cried. "Why did you keep running after they caught your fly ball? Why did you run past Philip and Ronald and knock Janet over?"

"Yeah, are you crazy?" Philip shouted.

Janet was dusting herself off.

Ronald was really mad. He shot me a dirty look and said, "Why didn't you do what Mr. Duggins told you?"

"Yeah, we would have won, Roxanne!" Abby threw her bat down and kicked it aside. She let out a long exasperated sigh and headed out to first base.

We went into extra innings to break the tie. We tried our hardest to contain them, but Edgebrook was on a roll. With two out and two strikes, their shortstop hit a solid grounder in between first and second. The girl on third made it into home safely and scored.

When it was our turn to bat, Abby hit a fly ball

right into the glove of their second baseman. She was followed by the Pilcher twins who both struck out. The final score was Edgebrook 13, Lazy Hills 12.

Afterward, there was a big awards ceremony. The Edgebrook coach, Buster Jones, was awarded the Coach of the Year trophy. Mad Dog tried to be a good sport and even shook Buster's hand, but when he looked at me, I could see that the gleam in his eyes was missing. Then Claudia's mom ran onto the field in a gorgeous blue dress and interviewed Buster for the "Live at Five" news.

After the ceremony, the crowd poured onto the field.

"I think you were very brave," Mom said to me. "Why, just standing up there in front of all those people took courage."

"Mom!" I cried. "Anybody can stand up at the plate. It takes a real dope to try and hit a ball when all you need is a crummy walk."

"Well, at least you tried," Mom said. Then she leaned over and gave me a squeeze. I know she was trying to help, but a squeeze from Mom in front of Claudia and everybody was embarrassing.

Then Dad said, "Don't feel bad, Roxanne. I was playing football once and ran the wrong direction for a touchdown. I ended up scoring the winning point for the *other* team! So you see, this sort of thing happens to the best of us."

"Likely story, Dad," I said.

"Believe it or not, it's true."

Trip didn't say a word. He looked at me and shook his head like he couldn't believe he had such a dopey sister.

A little later, Mr. Duggins pulled me over and told me it wasn't my fault. He said he hoped I didn't feel responsible, which made me feel worse—like a traitor. If I hadn't been trying to show Claudia up by being a superstar, we would have won.

Then he insisted we all pile into his white convertible and go to the Burger Barn.

Mad Dog tried to act cheerful but he didn't fool me. He ordered cheeseburgers and chocolate malts for all of us, but just coffee for himself. And he didn't play Twenty Questions with us or tell us a *Mad Men from Mars* story. He didn't even mention the game.

Normally I love the way Joe's cheeseburgers melt in your mouth. But now my throat felt all dry. It was hard to swallow. My cheeseburger tasted like a thick piece of cardboard. I tried to wash it down with the malt.

"Are you sure you don't want a *hot dog*," said Abby icily. She moved far away from me and sat next to Janet, near the jukebox.

I felt really bad. I wanted to make everything all right again. I wanted to make Mad Dog forget about the game. So I tried to think of something that would cheer him up. Then I remembered what Trip had told me about the Book Fair that Mr. Duggins always put on in November. I was sure once he started talking about books, he would feel better.

I slid off my stool and walked over to him. He was staring off into space.

"Mr. Duggins, I can't wait for school to start on Monday," I said. "Will you be dressing up as a famous fictional character on the first day? Will you be playing Twenty Questions with us during lunch? I'll bet we have the best Book Fair ever this year."

". . . what?" he asked.

"You know, Twenty Questions . . . school . . . fifth grade . . ."

"I don't know, Roxanne," he said, sighing. "I can't really think about that now."

"Sure, I understand," I said. "Well, I'd better go. I just wanted to let you know I'm really excited about having you for a teacher. It's going to be a great year."

I went outside and sat in the backseat of Mr. Duggins's convertible. For a while, I counted all the blue squares on the upholstery. Then I tried counting the stars, but I kept losing track because my eyes were watery and it was hard to see them clearly. I wished Monday would hurry up and come.

Monday morning started off with a bang. I was taking a bite of oatmeal when Mom got the phone call.

While she talked, I scooped the last raisin out of my oatmeal. Mom had gotten up extra early to make it for me, which would have been fine if it had been the middle of winter and I was used to eating early. As it was, I felt nervous enough without having to look at something that sat in the bowl all lumpy and gooey and looked like "The Living Brain."

"Good grief," she cried. She banged the receiver down and started running around the kitchen. "I had to reschedule my audition for ten-thirty this morning!"

"Why?" I asked. "Weren't you scheduled for after work?"

"Yes," she said, exasperated. "That Mr. Clown! You should have heard his temper tantrum and all because I asked him to tape his 'Happy Hour' thirty minutes early today. Well, he just refuses! Now the only time the camera crew can film me is this morning." She looked down at her blouse and cried, "I have to change. These stripes will drive our cameraman crazy!"

I guess she saw the panicked look on my face, because she tried to make a joke out of it.

"As the announcers say, don't go away. I'll be right back."

"Mom, I'm old enough to walk to school. Besides, I can't be late for my first day."

"I intend to take you to school on your first day until you start junior high." She was all emotional and her voice sounded shaky.

She hurried out of the kitchen and down the hall. "Don't worry, I'll be ready in plenty of time," she called.

While Mom was gone, I dumped the oatmeal back into the pot, then tried to nibble on a piece of toast. I couldn't stop thinking about how I had messed up the game, and not just any game, the Pony League Championship. And to make matters worse, Abby was still mad at me. Before the game, we had agreed to watch the beginning of the "I Love Lucy" festival on Channel Six at her house. But yesterday when I went over, she poked her head out the door and said she was busy. I know she was watching it, though, because I could hear Lucy's and Ethel's voices in the background.

Then I started thinking about Mr. Duggins, trying

to remember everything Trip had told me about him. I guess I sort of drifted off, because when I glanced at the clock, it was already fifteen minutes to eight. I heard Mom in her bedroom and hurried back to see what was keeping her.

She was in the closet, throwing dresses out onto the bed.

"Roxanne, you've got to help me," she moaned. "It's between these two, I think." She pointed to a beige knit dress and a dark gray jumper with a white blouse.

I reached into her closet and pulled out the bright purple blouse Dad had given her last Christmas.

She held it up and looked at her reflection in the closet mirror.

"I don't know," she said hesitantly. "It's awfully bright. And what skirt would I wear with it?"

"It's just what you need," I said, remembering how Claudia's mom had looked. "Trust me."

"What I need is to have my head examined," she said, slumping onto the bed. She glanced at her watch. "Good grief, I'm running out of time. I'll have to take all of these and decide at the studio." She started gathering up the dresses.

"I'll meet you in the car," I yelled over my shoulder.

"Don't forget to brush your hair," she called back.

It was ten minutes to eight when we backed out of the driveway. Mom sped around the corner like a race-car driver. On the turn at Elm Street, our tires squealed. That scared Mom because she slowed right down.

We were practically crawling when we pulled into the little asphalt turnaround in front of school.

Just seeing the old school made me feel better. And I couldn't help thinking that even though Claudia's school, Edgebrook Academy, is newer and shinier, I like Lazy Hills better. I love the way the worn bricks feel smooth under my sneakers and how the wooden floor catches my reflection and how Mrs. Tetter's library smells like lemon oil.

"Did you brush your hair?" Mom asked, giving me a once-over.

"I forgot," I said.

She shook her head. "Roxanne, we already discussed this. It's up to you to make sure your socks match and your hair is brushed and if you don't, well . . ."

"I'll have to suffer the consequences, I know, Mom," I said quickly. "My hair is fine."

"All right," she said, "have a good day, Roxanne." She leaned over to kiss me.

"Mom!" I cried.

"What?" She looked shocked. "Did I forget something?"

"Mom," I said, rolling my eyes.

"Oh, that's right, you're too old." She lowered her voice in mock seriousness. "Good luck," she said. Then she shook my hand.

"Very funny, Mom," I said, getting out of the car.

The corners of Mom's mouth were turning up in a grin. The look on her face made me laugh.

"I hope you win," I called, as she pulled away from the curb.

I had to race inside and hurry to the second floor. I didn't have time to feel the steps or notice the floor or anything. I just made it to room 211 when the five-minute warning bell rang.

I stopped outside the door and smoothed my rumpled hair.

Something was wrong. For one thing, no sound was coming from the fifth-grade classroom.

Mr. Duggins was sitting behind his oak desk. He wasn't dressed in a costume. Instead, he was wearing gray slacks, a white dress shirt, and shiny black shoes.

"Won't you take a seat?" he said, as if he hardly knew me.

There were two empty seats, one in front of Ronald and one in the very back of the room. Abby hadn't saved me a seat. It may not sound like a big deal, but we've had this agreement since second grade: The first one in the room saves the other one a seat. When Abby saw me, she shrugged her shoulders and wrinkled her nose. She had a guilty look on her face.

"Hey, Rox, rest your socks," whispered Ronald. He scooted out the chair with his feet.

"Thanks, I'd rather sit in front, anyway," I said, loudly enough for Abby to hear.

Mr. Duggins didn't say a word about the Book

Fair. Instead, we spent the morning passing out dusty old textbooks. By noon, I was starving.

I hurried through the lunch line and picked a cheese sandwich, mashed potatoes, and milk. Abby was ahead of me. When I reached the table I was shocked. Abby hadn't saved me a seat. I didn't look at her as I sat down at the other side of the table next to Janet and some of the other kids. While we were waiting for Mr. Duggins to come and play Twenty Questions, I noticed my entire lunch was off-white. In my best vampire voice I said, "Look, Abby, 'A Lunch from the Murky Beyond.' "

I happened to think it was pretty funny. Ronald and Philip laughed. But Abby turned away.

"Hey, where's Mad Dog going?" Janet asked.

Mr. Duggins walked past our table on his way to the far side of the lunchroom.

"Hey, Mr. Duggins," I called. "Aren't you going to play Twenty Questions with us?"

"No," he called back.

When he reached the wall, he leaned over, rolled out a straw mat, and sat down.

"Oh, great," Abby said. "Thanks a lot, Roxanne."

"Me? What did I do?"

"If you hadn't been showing off, we would have won the game and Mr. Duggins would be Coach of the Year. Instead, he's acting weird."

"That's not fair." I could feel my face growing hot.

"Yes it is," Abby said. "Thanks to you, Mr. Duggins feels like a loser." She folded her arms across her chest, leaned back in her chair, and glared at me.

"Don't worry, Abby," I said. "I'll make it up to him. I'll make it up to everybody. I'll think of a way."

"That's what I'm worried about," Abby told Philip.

Philip turned in his chair. "Now, Lucy," he said, shaking his finger at me.

Ronald and Abby started laughing.

"Very funny," I said. They were still laughing as I shoved my chair under the table. I stood as far away from them as possible during clean-up. I scraped my plate, stacked my tray, and got in line by the door. After a while, Abby came up behind me. I turned my head away so I wouldn't have to talk to her. Luckily, Mr. Duggins came right over and led us to the library to check out biographies for our first assignment.

I figured when we got to the library Mr. Duggins would be his old self again. After all, besides baseball, books are his passion. He really gets into them. Before he even reads a page, he runs his hands over the jackets, opens them up, and takes a deep sniff. He's practically famous for running around the library, tearing from shelf to shelf, grabbing books and crying, "You'll love this! Fantastic! Hilarious! Rip-roaring fun!" But today, Mr. Duggins walked right past the bookshelves. He walked over to the audio section, pulled out a cassette, and plugged in a headset.

Abby gave me one of her I-told-you-so looks. I walked right past her and sat at the back table, across from the first-grade classroom. I took a deep

25

breath and got a big whiff of Mrs. Tetter's lemon oil. Then I leaned over and watched the first-graders. Their little faces were scrubbed and smiling. They looked so innocent listening to their teacher read a book. Just watching them made me feel weird, like I'd been split in half or something. Half of me missed Abby and wanted her back as my best friend. The other half was angry at her. She shouldn't blame me if Mr. Duggins acted weird. And what did she expect me to do at the game, ignore Claudia while she made fun of my mom and me? Nobody makes fun of a Bookman and gets away with it! If Abby was a true friend, she'd be understanding. She'd stick by me, no matter what.

I walked up to Mrs. Tetter's desk. Philip and Abby were in line ahead of me. Philip was holding books about two famous baseball players, Ty Cobb and, of course, Reggie Jackson. Abby had just set down an armload of biographies about Marie Curie and Eleanor Roosevelt. I had one on the life of Amelia Earhart.

"Mrs. Tetter," I whispered.

She glanced up from the books and pushed her glasses into her brown hair.

"Yes, Roxanne?"

"What's *really* the matter with Mr. Duggins?"

"I wouldn't presume to say," she said. "Of course, we all have things about ourselves we'd like to change. I do. Don't you?"

"Yes, don't you, Roxanne?" asked Abby, glaring at me.

For the first time ever, I think I hated Abby. I cleared my throat and looked right at Mrs. Tetter.

"Not me," I said in my best sarcastic voice. "All I care about is winning. Do you have any good books on the subject?"

Abby gathered up her books in a huff and walked out the door with Janet. I stayed in the library while Mrs. Tetter pulled down books about winning and stacked them on a table. Then I picked through them and settled on one called *Five Easy Steps to Winning*.

After school, I waited by the outside door for Abby. I wanted to explain my side of what had happened during the game, but she was nowhere in sight. I tucked the Amelia Earhart biography and *Five Easy Steps to Winning* under my arm and ran all the way home.

When I got there, the house was quiet. I checked the back bedroom but Mom wasn't there, so I put the books on her bedside table and sat down.

I tried to think of a way to make it up to Mr. Duggins and the team, but my thoughts were all jumbled. When I thought about Abby, I felt lonely and sad and mad.

Then I started thinking about Mom being the new host of a TV show. I can't really explain it, except to say that the thought of having to share Mom with about a zillion people just made me feel more lonely. And I'm not proud of this, but I started hoping that she'd lose. After all, I'd lost my best friend. The least Mom could do was be home for me.

Tuesday was worse than Monday. All day, Mr. Duggins was quiet and glum and barely talked above a whisper. By the time the final bell rang, I felt so bad, I was afraid I would start crying. I guess Abby noticed because she waited for me by the door.

"Sorry I've been so mean," she said. "But sometimes you make me crazy."

"Sometimes you make me crazy, too," I said. Then I made my famous Lucy face. I opened my green eyes real wide and sucked in my cheeks. Abby broke out laughing.

She and Janet had made plans for just the two of them to walk down the hill to the big public library, but they asked me to come along.

When we got there, Janet searched for biographies of Mary McLeod Bethune and Abby and I flipped through fashion magazines. We were laughing at the dopey expressions on some of the models when Claudia and a small group of girls walked in.

I buried my head in the magazine and hoped she wouldn't notice me. But she walked right over and bumped the back of my chair.

"Hey, Roxanne, guess what?" she asked, loudly enough for the other girls to hear. "We have the *best* teacher. She's *so* pretty. Too bad you're stuck with weird old Mr. Duggins."

"Mr. Duggins is great," I said. "He's really fun!" Abby looked at me like I was from outer space. I stared back down at the magazine, hoping Claudia would walk away. Instead, she leaned on the back of my chair.

"Oh, and another thing," she whispered. "The best mother won!"

"What do you mean?"

"You'll see," she said. Then she whispered something to her friends and they all started laughing.

As we were walking home, Janet asked me, "What did Claudia whisper to you?"

"I don't remember," I lied. "She thinks she's so great."

"Well, she is pretty and she does have a lot of friends," said Abby.

"So?"

"So, there must be a good side to her that we just don't know."

Janet nodded her head in agreement.

"If there is, I'd like to see it," I said.

After we dropped Janet off, it was still early. I went over to Abby's to watch some of the "I Love Lucy" festival. Before it started, we caught the tail end of a special about the Bermuda Triangle. Some guy was explaining about people who were zapped; they existed one day and were mysteriously gone the next. It reminded me of Mad Dog. It reminded Abby, too.

"Maybe Mr. Duggins went to Bermuda last weekend," she said.

"He's zapped, all right," I said.

After the special, one of my favorite "Lucy" episodes came on. It was the one where Lucy and Ethel were working on an assembly line in a candy factory. Their job was to put chocolate bonbons into packages. They were doing fine until the conveyor belt went crazy, and candy started zooming past them at about a zillion miles an hour. They couldn't package the candy fast enough, so they popped the bonbons into their mouths and hid them under their caps.

Abby was laughing her head off, but I couldn't concentrate. When I looked at the screen, I kept seeing the faces of Mr. Duggins, Mom, and Claudia. What did Claudia mean about the best mother winning?

I found out later. On "Live at Five" they announced that Suzy Slooder was the new host of "Around Town."

Dad was upset. "I'm going to call that station and give them a piece of my mind," he said.

"Don't you dare!" Mom said. "In a way, I'm glad I didn't get the job. I probably would've killed myself or the children, rushing to work every day. And I'd never be home for them after school—not to mention dinner."

"Betsy, we could have made after-school arrangements. As for dinner, I love to cook. Besides, we Bookmans stick together. We would have pitched in and helped."

We watched the first "Around Town" on Thursday night. Dad sat next to Mom on the couch and held her hand. Trip and I sat on the floor in front of the TV.

"Welcome to 'Around Town,' the show that looks for the best in everything," Suzy said. She was beaming. "Tonight we are looking for the best cheeseburger in town and we're going to start right here!" She turned around and pointed to the Burger Barn.

While Suzy was interviewing Joe, Mom told Dad how the show operated.

"It takes a lot of research," she said. "First someone has to do the homework, so Suzy can ask the right questions on Thursday. And it's a lot of work because it's a two-part show. On Friday, Suzy has to make a decision and pick the best. I wouldn't want to be in her shoes."

"But she doesn't have to do it all by herself, does she?" Dad asked.

"Of course not," Mom said. "Television is a team effort."

"Shh," said Trip. "I want to hear this." He turned up the volume.

"Next week, we will be looking for the best teacher," Suzy said. "If you have a teacher you'd like to nominate, please call me at 555-WINS. That's 555-WINS."

When I heard her say that, a light bulb went off inside my head. I felt my green eyes widen. I was glad Abby wasn't sitting next to me. She knows I get that look when I'm about to do something daring.

While Mom and Dad talked to Trip, I ran upstairs. Suzy Slooder had given me the perfect plan.

Quietly, I pulled the hall phone into my room and locked the door. My fingers were shaking as I dialed the number. Suzy answered on the fourth ring.

"Hi, I'm Roxanne Bookman," I said. "And have I got a teacher for you."

When I told Abby about my plan, she said we should work on getting the old Mad Dog back. During the second week of school, we tried asking him about famous people. Then we tried bringing him baseball cards. Still, Mr. Duggins was moody and unhappy and not at all his normal self.

On the morning of the interview he came around to the front of his desk wearing a strange baggy white jacket and pants. I guess his outfit was supposed to look cool, but it reminded me of pajamas. I was beginning to regret having nominated him. He pushed up his sleeves and patted his forehead with a white handkerchief. Then he gave a little speech.

"Class, Mrs. Tetter tells me that some of you are concerned about me. A few weeks ago, I discovered there are some things about myself I'd like to change. Then I stumbled across this fabulous cassette called *Inner Peace: Meditation Techniques*." He turned around, picked it up from his desk, and held it up for us to see. "Today, I thought we'd try one of the meditation exercises."

Most of the kids looked puzzled or embarrassed. I glanced up at the clock over the door. All I could think about was Suzy Slooder. Her "Around Town" crew was due to arrive at any moment. I wanted to go up and warn Mr. Duggins, but I couldn't. It was against the "Around Town" rules.

"Philip, please get the lights," Mr. Duggins said. "Class, I'd like you to close your eyes and rest your hands on your desks, palms up."

Abby and I looked at each other and rolled our eyes at about the same time. Then we broke out laughing.

"Take some deep breaths," said Mr. Duggins softly. "Imagine that your life is a big blank movie screen. Your job is to fill that screen with pleasant images. Let's begin."

The classroom grew dark and strangely quiet. It was hot and stuffy. I closed my eyes and took a deep breath. I tried to concentrate, but images of Suzy Slooder and her crew kept popping up on my blank screen. I heard Abby clear her throat. After a while, I heard Ronald's breathing. It sounded slow and steady and when I turned around and looked, I noticed that he and several of the other kids were asleep.

Then Mr. Duggins flipped the lights back on. "Wasn't that refreshing?" he said.

I was relieved that it was finally lunchtime. The lunchroom was cool and relaxing. Abby and I were sitting down when we heard Mr. Duggins walking behind us. His feet made a funny scraping sound. Just hearing the sound made me feel better about everything.

"I'll bet he's trying to give us a clue," I whispered excitedly to Abby. "I know just who he's going to be. Frankenstein, of course."

I couldn't think of anyone else who walked with that shuffling sound. It reminded me of the way I sounded when I was three and had tied two wooden sanding blocks to the bottoms of my shoes to make me taller. Naturally, I was curious to see if Mr. Duggins had done the same thing, so I looked down at his feet.

The shiny black tie-up shoes he'd been wearing since school started were gone. So were his socks. I know it sounds weird, but he was wearing red plastic slippers with little spikes all over them. They were the Ultra Massage Slippers advertised for $7.95 on Channel Six. The idea behind them was that the spikes were supposed to massage your bare feet and help you relax. Trip said they looked like some sort of medieval torture. He said they probably worked, since they made your feet hurt so much you didn't have time to worry about anything else.

It would have been all right if the slippers and pajamas were the whole problem. But Mr. Duggins shuffled over to his mat, closed his eyes, and started humming loudly. I crossed my fingers and hoped Suzy Slooder would forget about the interview.

We were still eating when she arrived. I had expected her crew to consist of a dozen or so people running around, all dressed up and glamorous. As it turned out, there were only two people on the "Around Town" crew: a cute, adorable, awesome, incredibly gorgeous guy carrying a camera over his right shoulder, and a girl who was in charge of lights and microphones.

Suzy ran right into our table.

"How can you see in here? It's so dark and gloomy," she said.

That was a surprise to me since I'd always thought of it as a cheerful place. I guess the girl agreed with Suzy, because she went out for more lights. Suzy waited awhile and then started without her.

"Hello, this is Suzy Slooder," she said, looking straight into the camera. "This afternoon, we are visiting Lazy Hills Elementary School where Mr. Walter Duggins, the fifth-grade teacher, has been nominated as the best teacher 'Around Town.' "

It was hard to hear her because of the humming. She must have noticed it, too, because she stopped and banged her microphone against our lunch table a couple of times. Any one of us could have told her it wouldn't help. We all knew the source of the humming.

"Are you in Mr. Duggins's fifth-grade class?" Suzy leaned over and stuck the microphone under Abby's chin. Then the cameraman wheeled around and aimed the lens at her nose. Abby stared straight into the camera, speechless.

"I'm Roxanne Bookman," I said quickly.

"Hello, Roxanne, nice to meet you." Suzy Slooder shook my hand. "Why do you think Mr. Duggins is such a special teacher?"

"Well," I said. "For one thing, he's different. He's enthusiastic and fun and never boring."

"Wonderful words of praise," she said into the camera. "But now, let's see for ourselves, shall we?"

She aimed the microphone under Ronald's chin. "Could you tell me where I might find Walter Duggins?"

"You mean Mad Dog?"

"Mad Dog?" Suzy repeated. "Who is Mad Dog?"

"Oh, did I say Mad Dog?" Ronald cried, blushing.

"He meant Mr. Duggins." Philip pointed. The cameraman followed the direction of Philip's finger over to Mr. Duggins. He was still sitting on the mat, humming.

The cameraman zoomed back to Suzy.

"That's your teacher?" she asked.

Abby, Ronald, and Philip turned to me.

I nodded yes.

Suzy hurried over and interviewed Mr. Duggins. Abby and I watched for a while. It seemed to be going poorly; Mr. Duggins kept looking down at his feet.

After school, Abby was waiting for me by the door.

"Mr. Duggins didn't do too well, did he?" I asked.

"No, he sure didn't."

"Maybe we just think he looked bad because we're not used to his new self," I said.

"Yeah, maybe," said Abby. "Besides, my mom says that the camera can do a lot to make people look better. She says that if you saw some of the Hollywood stars on the street, you probably wouldn't even recognize them."

"I hope you're right," I said.

When I got home, I told Mom and Trip about our class being on "Around Town."

"But it's no big deal," I said. "We don't even have to watch it."

"Of course we'll watch it," said Mom. "Let me call your father, so he can be home in time."

After Mom hung up the phone, I called Abby and invited her over to watch "Around Town" with us.

The segment came on at the very end of the "Live at Five" news show. Dad made it home just in time. Trip plopped himself down on the couch, next to Mom and Dad. Abby and I sat cross-legged on the floor.

"Turn it up," Trip said.

Suzy opened the show with an outside shot of Edgebrook Academy. It was new and modern-looking and about ten times bigger than Lazy Hills. Inside, instead of having plain wooden floors like we do, they had carpeting in this soft rose-colored hue. Their student lounge was awesome! It had cushioned chairs next to a huge picture window. On one side, there were ferns in hanging baskets, and on the other, there was an aquarium filled with brightly colored tropical fish. All we have is a couple of folding chairs in the nurse's room.

The next shot showed the inside of the fifth-grade classroom. It was obvious from the way everyone looked that the school was air-conditioned. I thought I spotted Claudia in the back of the room, sitting stiff and still. Her teacher, Miss High, looked great on TV. She looked like she could have been on the cover of *Teacher of the Year* magazine. She was young, with black hair and soft brown skin, and she had a sweet smile.

"I'd just like to say, I'm so honored to be nominated." She gazed calmly into the camera. "Of course, it would be wonderful to win," she continued. "But really, teaching these precious children is its own reward."

"Nauseating," cried Trip. "She probably practiced that all week!"

"Trip!" Dad warned.

Abby nudged me in the ribs and we both started to laugh.

We got quiet when Lazy Hills came on. Our lunchroom looked small and dark and gloomy. Then Abby's face flashed in front of the screen.

"Oh no! I look like a zombie!" Abby squealed.

"No, you don't," I lied.

Then my face came on the screen. I think I was staring too hard at the camera or something, because my eyes were crossed. My voice was high and squeaky.

"What's that buzzing sound?" Dad asked.

"We're getting to that," I said.

The camera swung around and caught several kids making goofy faces before it landed on Mr. Duggins. His eyes were closed and he was humming. He seemed to be in a trance.

I looked at Mom and Dad. Dad seemed tense but Mom didn't seem too worried yet. I guess she thought someone on Suzy's crew had done some homework, and that Suzy would ask Mr. Duggins about the Book Fair, or his unique philosophy of teaching. But Suzy just stood there, holding the microphone under his nose.

"I don't know what to say," Mr. Duggins said, looking away from the camera. "I don't think that teaching should be competitive. There shouldn't be a winner or a loser. What we need is more cooperation among schools." Then he looked down. The camera followed his glance and focused on his Ultra Massage Slippers.

Suzy's voice was upbeat.

"Well," she said, "this has been such an exciting

day—two terrific teachers! But only one will be the winner. Please tune in tomorrow as we make the educated choice and announce the best teacher 'Around Town.' "

I felt terrible. I was angry at Mr. Duggins for making a mess of the interview and even madder at myself for nominating him in the first place.

"I just wish they'd done their homework and asked him about all his innovative programs," Mom said. "Still, he didn't do too badly."

"It was a nightmare, a disaster. He blew it," I cried. "It was as if he wanted to lose!"

"I liked what he said about cooperation," Mom said.

"You would, Mom. You don't understand anything about winning," I said, before I could stop myself.

"Roxanne!" Dad warned.

"Well, Dad, she doesn't!"

"Roxanne, that's enough!"

"If she knew anything about winning, she'd be the host of 'Around Town,' instead of Suzy Slooder!"

Dad turned to Abby. "Abigail," he said, "I'm glad you could come but I think you'd better run on home now."

"I'll walk you," I said quickly.

"I don't think that's necessary," Dad said.

I walked Abby to the door. My knees were shaking. Abby could tell that I was in trouble. She said, "Don't blame yourself. At least you tried!"

Dad kept a thin smile on his face until Abby was

out the door. Then he turned to me and said, "Go to your room, young lady!"

"Gladly," I said. Then I raced up the stairs two at a time.

A little later, Mom came into my bedroom. She was carrying a tray with a ham sandwich, a glass of milk, and the library books I had left in her room.

"I thought you might be hungry," she said, placing the tray on my bedside table. She sat down beside me on the bed.

"I'm sorry," I said quietly. "I didn't mean those things. Sometimes I say things without really thinking." I sat up in bed, leaned over, and hugged her.

"That's all right," she said. "Sometimes I do things without thinking, too!"

"You? That's funny, Mom. You never make mistakes."

"I have a little secret," she said. "Do you promise not to tell?"

I nodded yes. She leaned over closer to me and lowered her voice. "You know that audition I told everyone I lost. Well, the truth is I didn't even go. And it's not because I didn't want to win, it's because I was afraid of losing."

"But, Mom," I cried. "You should've gone. You're really good at TV."

"I know I should have tried," she said. "And I was fine up until the last minute. Then I sort of chickened out. It's something I've been trying to work on.

I guess I need this, huh?" She picked up *Five Easy Steps to Winning* and started flipping through the pages. "Seriously," she said. "Would you mind if I borrowed it? I might pick up some pointers."

I blushed and felt embarrassed, like I had during Mr. Duggins's little speech to our class. What was the matter with all the grown-ups?

"Sure, take it," I said.

She tucked the book under her arm, then gave me a good-night kiss and hurried back downstairs. I hadn't realized how hungry I was, but as soon as she left, I ate most of the sandwich and drank the milk.

I was just getting out of bed to turn off the light when Trip came in.

"You're the idiot who nominated Mr. Duggins, aren't you?" he said, picking through the leftover sandwich.

"How did you know?"

"Because I did some stupid things when I was your age, too."

"Nothing as stupid as I've done," I said, sliding back under the covers.

"Oh yeah? What about the time I convinced our Pony League team to have Mom and Dad as our coaches?" He was smiling. "Even you'd never do anything that stupid."

"What did happen?" I asked, sitting up in bed. "I've been dying to know."

"Well," Trip said. "Dad drove everyone crazy with

the rule book. And Mom got us all so nervous, we practically freaked out at the play-offs. You should have seen her. She was frightening!"

"Wow! That sounds pretty bad."

"It was bad, all right. I don't even like to think about it." He sighed and shook his head. "Well, you'd better get some sleep. You'll need it!"

"Good night."

Trip turned out the light and left the room.

After he was gone, I slid down between the covers. Just knowing that Trip and Mom had made mistakes made me feel better. I drifted right off to sleep.

In the morning, our class went to Edgebrook to check out the possibility of using their facilities for the Book Fair. Mr. Duggins got the idea when he saw their media center on "Around Town." Our class waited for Miss High in the principal's office. The office was shiny and polished and smelled like the inside of a new car. The secretaries were talking about Miss High and betting that she would win the Best Teacher Award.

Although I hated to admit it, Miss High was really nice. She let us stop and admire the tropical fish. Then she led us into the media center and taught us how to write our names on the computers. I spaced each letter out so my name covered the whole page. While we worked, I overheard Miss High talking to Mr. Duggins.

"Have you heard about the new 'Brain Teaser' contest on Channel Six? My fifth-graders are just raring to compete and show off all they've learned. I think it's great. Finally, something that's fun, and educational, too! How about it? Would your class be interested in competing against mine?"

"Oh, I don't think . . ." said Mr. Duggins, his voice trailing off. I didn't hear the rest because there was a loud clatter as the Edgebrook fifth-graders came into the room.

Claudia Slooder brushed past Abby and stood in front of me.

"Too bad *your* teacher isn't going to beat *our* teacher," she said. "What's his name again, Puppy Dog?" The girls in the group started laughing.

"It's Mr. Duggins to you," I said. "And you don't know who won."

"Oh yeah? Roxanne, face it, you guys at Lazy Hills are losers." The other fifth-graders nodded their heads in agreement.

"We're not losers!" I cried.

"Ignore her," Abby whispered in my ear.

"Really, then prove it!" Claudia stood with her hand on her hip.

"Okay, I will!"

"I'm waiting."

"Roxanne, forget it," Abby said.

I don't know what happened next, except to say that I started feeling strange. My head felt all cottony, my heart started thumping like mad, and I said, "Okay, I'll prove it. We challenge you to the 'Brain Teaser' show."

Suddenly, the room was quiet. Everyone was staring at me.

"Wonderful," Miss High exclaimed. She turned to Mr. Duggins, but he had already started toward the door.

Abby and I didn't talk until we reached the activity bus.

"What did you expect me to do?" I asked Abby. "I had to stand up to her."

"But the 'Brain Teaser' contest?" she said. "I heard it's going to be really tough."

I sat down next to her on the backseat.

"Ah, we can beat 'em," I said, with forced enthusiasm.

"We?" Abby said. "Oh, no. I'm not going back on TV. I looked like a zombie!"

"But you have to help me. You're my best friend. If you don't help me, who will?" I cried.

Abby had her arms folded squarely in front of her. She wouldn't budge.

"It's not going to be me. No way. Not in a billion, trillion years," she said. "You're going to have to get out of this mess all by yourself, Roxanne!"

The first thing Monday morning, Mr. Duggins had our class sign a note to Miss High, congratulating her for winning the Best Teacher Award. Then he picked up a memo that had been sent over from Channel Six. It outlined the rules of the "Brain Teaser" show. He motioned me up to his desk.

"Roxanne, why don't you read this to the class?"

I turned and looked out over the room. Ronald had his arms folded across his stomach and most of the other kids were slumped down in their chairs. Abby shoved a pencil behind her left ear and leaned forward. I took a deep breath and read the memo.

Congratulations for volunteering to partici-pate in the new Channel Six quiz show, "Brain Teaser." Your team will compete against Edge-brook Academy one week from Saturday. Please make a note of the following rules:

Each team will consist of four members, one to be designated as team captain. The captain will be responsible for any decision making

during the contest. The scoring will be as fol-
lows. During the first half, each correct answer
will be awarded one point, and during the
second half, each correct answer will be
awarded two points.

Over one hundred questions will be submit-
ted by a panel of impartial judges. The ques-
tions will cover the following categories:
history, English, social studies, math, science,
and miscellaneous.

A list of specific rules governing the contest
will be forwarded to your school. Coaches,
please review these rules carefully.

This program will be videotaped. We will
have a short rehearsal in the Edgebrook audi-
torium next Wednesday afternoon at 5:00 P.M.
The actual contest will begin at 10:00 A.M. Sat-
urday at Edgebrook. We ask that team mem-
bers report no later than 9:30 A.M.

"Brain Teaser" will be aired on our
expanded Saturday edition of "Live at Five."
Good Luck!

When I finished reading, I turned and looked at
Mr. Duggins.

"That's fine, Roxanne," he said. Then he motioned
me closer to his desk. "There isn't much time to prepare for the contest," he whispered. "If I were you, I'd
go ahead and pick the team today. You can practice

in the library each day after lunch." Then he turned toward the class.

"I'm going to make Roxanne the captain of the team," he said. "I want you to cooperate with her in any way you can." Then he went back to grading papers.

I wasn't sure if I was supposed to sit down or not, so I stood there for a while absorbing all the information. It was official. As captain of the team, it was my job to pick three other kids, ones who would be whizzes at history, English, social studies, math, and science. I wasn't sure about the miscellaneous section. I was trying to think of a system to pick the team, when a low rumbling came from the back of the room. Several kids were forming a huddle. Every once in a while, one of them would shoot me a poisonous look. It didn't take a genius to see that the class was turning ugly. I looked at Mr. Duggins. He smiled.

I cleared my throat.

"Don't forget," I told the class. "Mr. Duggins is going to coach us. Tell them, Mr. Duggins." I was sure he couldn't pass up this challenge. I expected him to get up and start pacing like he had during the play-off games. I expected to hear his booming voice say something like, "Let's toss this up and see how it flies." Instead, he looked puzzled as he pushed his chair back and stood up.

"Class, remember when I mentioned I was working

on changing some things about myself? Well, one of the things I'm working on is my competitive nature. I'm afraid I can't coach anymore. Whenever I do, I just go wild about winning."

I looked around the classroom for some sign of support. Ronald and Philip were passing notes. Abby was acting like she was engrossed in a book, but I knew she was pretending because it was upside down. I hurried back to my desk before someone threw something at me.

After lunch, we went to the library. While Mr. Duggins and Mrs. Tetter looked through book catalogs, I picked the team—Abby, Ronald, Philip, and me. I know it sounds like I picked my friends, but the truth is *nobody* wanted to be on the team. When I went around to the different tables in the library, the kids jumped up and rushed over to the shelves. When I headed for the shelves, they ran to Mrs. Tetter's desk and checked out books. Ronald, Philip, and Abby didn't want to be team members, either, but they were my friends—they couldn't duck out on me.

Mrs. Tetter must have noticed the desperate look on my face because she handed me a stack of books.

"Maybe the information in these will help your team get ready," she said.

Before dinner, Mom helped me prepare questions. I offered to bring down the books that Mrs. Tetter had given me, but Mom said she didn't need them. She spread a little set of baby encyclopedias out on the table. It was the set she got free at the grocery store when I was four. There are ten books in the set. It's called *Little Student's Magic World*. Just like real encyclopedias, the books are divided alphabetically. The problem is they're mostly pictures. For instance, under Florida it shows a giant picture of a palm tree. The text says: *Florida is a very big state. It is an arm of land surrounded on three sides by water. It is mostly a peninsula. Can you say* pen-in-su-la?

"I need something older," I told Mom.

"How about if I try to think back to when I was in the fifth grade. Then I'll just toss out some questions."

"That would be great, Mom." I was beginning to feel more optimistic.

Mom closed her eyes and thought for a long time.

"Um. Um. Okay. Okay," she said, opening her eyes. "Write this down. What's five times six?"

"Times?" I cried. "Mom, are you joking? We learned times in third grade."

"No problem," she said. She thought for another minute. "Okay, I've got another one!" she said excitedly. "What is Boyle's Law?" She was nodding her head up and down.

"What are you talking about?"

"All right, I'll give you a clue," she said. "Chemistry!" She raised her eyebrows. "Got it?"

"Chemistry?" I cried.

"You mean you haven't had chemistry yet?" she asked, with a shocked look on her face.

"Of course not, Mom. I'm in the fifth grade."

"Sorry, I guess my fifth grade wasn't too memorable," Mom said, sighing.

I felt so hollow and empty inside, I thought eating might make me feel better.

"Come on, Mom," I said. "I'll help you make dinner."

I washed the lettuce and tossed the salad while Mom fried chicken. I must have been starving, because I ended up having two helpings of everything. I felt much better until Mom told Dad about helping me. Then he volunteered.

"How about a couple of word problems?"

Trip kicked me under the table. He shook his head no, then put his hand up to his throat and stuck out his tongue. It was hard to keep from laughing. Being an engineer makes Dad think everyone loves word problems.

"Okay," I said, trying to sound enthusiastic.

"Good luck," Trip whispered.

"Trip!" Dad said sternly. "Isn't it your turn to wash the dishes?"

Trip started to clear the table while Dad and I went into the living room. We'd hardly sat down before Dad said, "Bill, Bob, and Jack are traveling. Bill's airplane is traveling at one half the speed of Jack's.

Bob's airplane is traveling at twice the speed of Bill's. All things being equal, which airplane will reach its destination first? Second? Third?"

"Are they propeller planes or jets?" I asked.

"It doesn't matter."

"Well, where are they going?"

"That doesn't matter, either," Dad said.

"Of course it matters," I cried. "Three men are traveling and they don't know what kind of airplanes they're on or where they're going?"

"I think you've missed the point." Dad was speaking in that carefully measured tone of voice he gets when he is starting to lose his patience.

We did three more word problems. Then Dad gave up and went into the kitchen to get a drink of water. I went to my room. I spread the books that Mrs. Tetter had given me on the floor. After two hours of studying and writing questions, I realized that I was not a typical fifth-grader. The more I read, the more nervous I became. My paper ripped. My pencil broke. My throat started to feel all tight and squeezed together, and my eyes started stinging. I looked up just as Trip passed my room.

"Could you please help me?" I said.

He peered into my room and gazed at the books strewn all over the floor and my crumpled paper.

"The trouble with you is you're such a baby," Trip said. "Here, let me look." He yanked the paper from my hand. "These questions don't make any sense."

By then, the stinging in my eyes had turned into tears. I tried to brush them away before Trip saw them, but they were coming too fast.

Trip looked at me and let out a long sigh.

"Oh, all right, I'll help. But I'm only going to write a few."

We worked until we had ten each.

"Thanks," I said. "You've saved my life."

"Don't I know it!" Trip said.

In the morning, there was another list of twenty-five questions. They were in Mom's handwriting. I gathered up all the questions and took them to school. Later, in the library, Abby, Ronald, and Philip joined me at the kindergartners' table. Abby leaned back in her chair and folded her arms. They were all grinning.

"We've been talking about the contest," Abby said. "We figure once Suzy Slooder gets a good look at our team during rehearsal, she'll remember how terrible we were on TV, and she'll call the whole thing off."

"Yeah, and we'll still get out of a lot of schoolwork while we practice," Ronald added.

"It'll be great," Philip said.

"Yeah, great." Secretly, I felt let down. I was hoping they'd want to beat Claudia and the kids at Edgebrook as badly as I did. Still, they hadn't refused to be on the team. I was sure they'd feel more competitive after we started practicing.

I asked the first set of questions. Mrs. Tetter seemed to be hunting for something, but I thought she was listening. I tried to assign them categories, based on how well they answered. Abby got ten out of forty-five right, if you count the fact that I gave her a point for knowing that the capital of Florida starts with a T. She also surprised me by describing bacteria correctly. I assigned her social studies and science.

Philip was the runner-up. He got four right, if you count his definition of an adjective. I made him responsible for English and math.

Ronald didn't seem to be feeling too well. "I'm not good at contests," he moaned. "I've never won anything."

Even so, he answered the first three questions correctly. He knew that the twentieth president was James Garfield. I gave him history.

The only remaining category was miscellaneous. I figured I would be good at this category, since I know a little bit about a lot of things.

"Who wrote those questions, anyway?" Abby asked. She was sore about missing some of the answers.

"Well, I wrote ten and . . ."

"No wonder." She snorted, then turned around in her chair.

"They are typical questions that *any* fifth-grader should know," I said.

Mrs. Tetter came over to our table and sat down.

"I couldn't help overhearing the questions," she said. "I think some of them were a little difficult to understand."

That's when I thought of a great idea.

"Mrs. Tetter, would you be our coach?"

"I'm sorry, I can't," she said. "I'm one of the judges. But, Roxanne, writing questions can be tricky. Did you write all of them?"

"Mom wrote twenty-five," I said, "and Trip wrote ten."

"Which ones did your mother write?"

I glanced over the list.

"That's funny," I said. "Most of the ones we answered correctly."

"Then why don't you ask your parents to coach?" Mrs. Tetter suggested.

"My parents? I don't think that's a good idea."

"Sure it is," Abby said. "Besides, you owe us."

"Well," I said, stalling. I remembered what Trip had said about Mom and Dad and coaching. Half of me wanted to heed his warning. The other half wanted to go ahead and ask them. I told myself it would work out fine, but somewhere deep inside I was afraid I was making my biggest mistake ever.

During dinner, I asked Mom and Dad if they would consider coaching our team. Trip dropped his fork and looked at me in disbelief. I tried not to look back at him.

Mom put her glass down.

"I don't know if I'm ready for something like that, Roxanne," she said.

"Of course you are, Betsy," Dad said. "Why, if you can audition in front of TV cameras, you can coach again."

Mom looked at me and blushed. I realized that she hadn't told Dad her secret.

"Come on, Mom," I urged. "We've just got to win!"

"Oh, all right," Mom said, laughing. "I'm sure it will be fine. Besides, I'm good at research," she added, more to herself than to us.

"Just don't come crying to me," Trip said, glaring.

"Trip! A Bookman forgives and forgets. Your play-offs were five years ago. That's a mighty long time to carry a grudge." Dad turned to me.

"Roxanne wants to have her parents for coaches, don't you, Roxanne?" Dad asked.

"Of course I do," I said. Still, I couldn't help thinking about Trip's warning.

I was up in my room, reading about how Amelia Earhart saved newspaper clippings about women in difficult professions, when I heard Mom in the attic.

"Where did you put your stopwatch—you know, the one you had in high school?" she yelled down to Dad.

"Isn't it with my old track clothes?" he hollered, racing up the stairs.

"Here's your clipboard. Oh Bill, look! My pink chiffon prom dress and your tux. Remember? And here are your track clothes!"

"I wonder if they still fit."

I squished my pillow up around my ears to block them out. I tried to imagine what it would be like having my parents as coaches. I pictured Mom asking multiplication facts in her pink chiffon prom dress while Dad read ridiculous word problems off his clipboard and paced back and forth in his old track clothes. It was not a pretty sight.

Mom met our team in the library after work on Thursday. Dad came in a few minutes later. Mrs. Tetter had cleared a little area for them behind the typewriter. She was working at her desk, flipping through the book catalogs and writing numbers on a piece of paper. I guess Trip was right about Dad because we spent forty-five minutes going over the rules.

"And remember, the answers are worth twice as many points in the second half," he declared in conclusion.

Then Mom got up holding *Five Easy Steps to Winning*.

"I've been reading this book," she said, "and I'd like to share it with you. According to this author, there are five easy steps to winning. First, you must know your goal."

"That's easy. We want to beat Edgebrook," called Philip.

"Very good," said Mom. "Second, you must be prepared. That's what we hope to accomplish by asking you practice questions. The third step is to be assertive. Does anyone know what that means?"

"It means being sure of yourself, I think," volunteered Abby.

"Very good," said Mom. "Let's take a minute and think about that."

I thought about Claudia and the championship game. She had acted so sure of herself. Maybe that's why she had won and I hadn't. She knew how to be assertive.

Mom continued. "The fourth step is to pinpoint your weaknesses. How would you go about pinpointing your weaknesses?"

Ronald raised his hand. He pointed to himself, then to Abby, Philip, and me. "There," he said. "I've pinpointed our weaknesses."

We all started laughing.

"Maybe if we go right on to the fifth step, you'll get a better idea! Turn your weaknesses into strengths. Any ideas on this one?"

"It could mean discovering something about yourself that keeps you from winning and then working to overcome it. All the baseball greats do that," said Philip.

"Excellent," Mom said. "Now, let's go right to the questions." She turned back to Dad.

He flipped through the pages on his clipboard. I hoped he would surprise me and ask something we knew, like a question about bacteria or the capital of California. Instead, he jumped right into one of his word problems.

"If one commuter train is traveling east at ten miles per hour loaded with potatoes from Idaho and a second commuter train is traveling west at ninety miles per hour with a load of tomatoes from Georgia, and the first commuter train derails outside of Pittsburgh, how much sooner than the first train will the second train reach its destination?"

There was silence. Mrs. Tetter looked up and shook her head.

"Roxanne, would you like to take it?" Dad asked.

I stalled. "Was the first train carrying potatoes or tomatoes?"

"I don't see that it makes any difference in the answer." He began drumming his fingers on the clipboard.

Then Ronald raised his hand.

"Are you talking about Pittsburgh, Pennsylvania? I went to Pittsburgh once and I didn't see any commuter trains with potatoes. Are you sure it was a commuter train?"

"I'm afraid you've all missed the point," Dad said. He was flustered.

I guess Mrs. Tetter noticed because she rushed over and whispered something to him.

"Perhaps I did leave a few things out," he mumbled.

He stepped back and Mom started asking her questions. She reviewed most of the twenty-five questions she had written and then asked some multiplication facts. They were easy. But we had trouble with her questions about Galileo. Mom seemed troubled, too. I guess she and Dad hadn't known what to expect from our team. Mrs. Tetter had a huddle with them and pointed them in the direction of the fifth-grade textbooks.

The next day, Mr. Duggins came to our practice. He sat cross-legged on the floor and smiled during Dad's questions. We were trying to do our best for Dad. And not just because he was our coach. It was plain to see that he and Mom wanted us to succeed. Mom, in particular, was really getting into it. Whenever Dad talked too long, she snapped her fingers.

He'd say, "Betsy, please," and she'd say, "Come on, come on. It's my turn."

We were just about through the science questions when Mrs. Tetter came over to my father and said, "Bill, you have a call. You can take it in the office."

While Dad was gone, Mom helped us review the states and their capitals. We were starting on the presidents and their vice-presidents when Dad came back. He stood quietly and listened to our run-through.

"Terrific!" said Dad. He turned to Mr. Duggins.

"Don't you agree?"

"Yes, a lovely job," said Mr. Duggins, smiling. He held Mom's and Dad's hands and looked down at his feet. Mom looked down, too. Mr. Duggins was still wearing his red plastic slippers.

Dad looked out over the team and beamed.

"I think we've come a long way," he said. "I'm proud of you." Then he turned to Mom and lowered his voice. "I'm afraid I have to go to Milwood right away. There's a problem with the bridge plans. I won't be back until Wednesday. Do you think you can handle this alone?"

"Of course," she said. "What could go wrong?"

7

Mom and Trip and I were watching "Live at Five" on Saturday when I realized we weren't the first "Brain Teaser" contestants. Milwood was competing against Northland. We'd beaten both towns in Pony League and I recognized some of the kids.

It was rugged. Suzy Slooder stood at a podium. Behind her was a big electronic timer. Team members sat at long tables equipped with four buzzers. The team that pressed the buzzer first had thirty seconds to answer. If they answered correctly, then Suzy went right on to the next question. If they missed, Suzy gave the opposing team thirty seconds to answer the same question. The terrifying part was when a team ran out of time. Then the timer started making this awful honking sound. Then Suzy went on to another question. Just watching the game made my stomach hurt. Mom was biting her fingernails before half-time.

After the last commercial, Suzy congratulated the Milwood team. Then she introduced the panel of judges. Mrs. Tetter came out onto the stage. Abby's mom was right about the camera making people look better. Mrs. Tetter looked terrific. It was hard to believe we knew her.

When the show was over, we sat down at the dining-room table to eat our chocolate pudding. Dad doesn't like it, so I only make it when he's away. I like to put it in our fancy glass goblets and heap whipped cream on top. Mom seemed preoccupied. She got up from the table and ran to her bedroom. When she came back, she was carrying the book on winning. She flipped to the third section.

"I think we need to be more assertive," she said, her spoon poised over the mound of whipped cream. "What do you think?"

I glanced over at Trip. He just shrugged and kept eating.

"I don't know, Mom," I said, looking down into my pudding.

"Of course you know!"

Her voice was getting louder and she was swirling her spoon around the goblet. It was flying so fast it made me dizzy.

"Yes, we definitely need to be more assertive," she said.

I looked at Trip and we both froze. I guess we thought if we sat really still, her mood would pass. We were wrong. It kept building. She hopped up from the table and pushed up her sleeves. Then she started pacing the floor.

"I've got it," she cried, slapping her forehead with the palm of her hand. "The basement. To the basement!"

She was definitely shouting now.

"What about the dishes?" I said.

"Forget 'em!" Mom cried. "Forget 'em!"

"I warned you," Trip said.

We followed Mom down the stairs.

By Monday, when the team met at my house after school, Mom had turned the basement into Operational Headquarters. She had the idea that we needed a special place where we wouldn't be distracted—a place where we could get down to the business of beating Edgebrook Academy.

It used to look like any other basement with an old sofa in the middle of the room, a beat-up black-and-white TV under a stack of newspapers, and a bunch of little collapsible TV trays. After Mom finished with it, the sofa was pushed up against the wall, the newspapers were gone, and the TV—with Dad's digital alarm clock on top—was dusted.

When the four of us reached the room, the TV was turned on and set to one of those VHS channels where the picture is all snow. The digital alarm was flashing zeros.

"This will simulate the electronic timer," Mom said, pointing to the alarm. "And this television will represent the video equipment that Channel Six will be using on Saturday when they tape the show.

Don't let it scare you. Just relax and pretend it's an old TV."

I don't think it scared any of us. After all, it *was* just an old TV. Mom had set up the four TV trays in front of the television. On the top of each tray was one of those little plastic clickers that are painted to look like bugs. They were leftover party favors from the kitchen drawer, where Mom keeps old water pistols, 3-D glasses, birthday candles, and that kind of stuff.

"These clickers will simulate the buzzers," Mom instructed us. "When you think you know the correct answer, PRESS THAT BUZZER!"

Mom was situated off to the side of the TV trays. She was standing behind something. I guess it was supposed to simulate a podium, but really—and this is the embarrassing part—it was my old high chair. Mom had put a piece of cardboard at a slant over the seat. On top of the cardboard were Dad's duck call and the wind-up egg timer I'd gotten her last Christmas. Mom was wearing Dad's sweatshirt and track shorts. While she flipped through a stack of questions, Ronald fiddled with the TV and Philip studied the digital clock. Then Abby traded her cricket clicker for Ronald's ladybug. They didn't seem too interested in practicing. In fact, Mom had to clap her hands twice to get their attention.

"This is a waste of time. When Suzy remembers us, she'll call it off before we ever get to rehearsal," Abby whispered to me.

"Give it a chance," I whispered back.

Mom set the egg timer and fired away.

I was having technical difficulties and couldn't get my clicker to work, so I missed the first ten questions. I kept raising my hand, but I couldn't get Mom to call on me, or take time out, or anything. She was acting frantic. She reminded me of someone.

I remembered a dream I'd had when I was in the fourth grade. I never told Mom or Dad about it. I was afraid they would take it the wrong way. The dream always started out the same. I would be sitting in my class minding my own business when suddenly, with no warning, Mom would be the teacher. In the first part of the dream, I would be tricked into thinking this was great. I would raise my hand and wiggle it wildly until I caught her attention. But as soon as she called on me, I would regret it. She would start off asking me embarrassing questions like, "Have you brushed your teeth?" Or she would say something like, "All this from a girl who leaves dirty socks under her bed?" Then she would make this clucking sound and turn into a giant chicken. I never did figure out what the dream meant. But I was always glad that Mom was my mom and not my teacher.

Suddenly, she made a loud honking sound with the duck call. It scared me so badly I jumped and knocked over the TV tray. I tried to grab it but it fell to the floor with a crash.

That's when Abby started laughing and Ronald asked if he could adjust the TV. Then Philip wanted to see if he could fix the digital clock. Abby asked Ronald if she could trade back the ladybug for the cricket.

"Let's settle down," Mom said. Her face was red and she was talking in that slow, measured way she gets when she is just about to blow her top. I think it's safe to say we all recognized the warning signs. I picked up the TV tray and repositioned my clicker. Then we all sat very still and looked straight ahead.

By the time Mom started another round of questioning, my clicker had loosened up and was working. We tried extra hard, and Mom seemed pleased. She was smiling. It was exhausting, though, with the egg timer going *ding* and the digital clock flashing. But the thing that really got me was the sound of the clickers. We sounded like a swarm of grasshoppers.

When we answered the last question, Abby's hair was hanging down in her eyes. Philip was slumped back in his chair, and Ronald had his head down on the TV tray. I felt all limp and crumpled. Mom looked the worst, though. I was surprised to see that she was smiling.

"Now we're going places," she said.

On Tuesday after school, Abby, Ronald, Philip, and I sat down behind our TV trays and Mom started firing questions at us. We were hitting the clickers and firing back answers in under thirty seconds.

"Let's move along a little faster," Mom cried. After three rounds of questions, she set the timer for twenty seconds.

"Mom!" I said. "They said in the rules we have thirty seconds to answer. I think you're getting carried away."

"Mrs. Bookman, I don't think we need the timer anymore," Abby said in a quiet voice.

"Abby's right," I said. "It's not like we're going to forget we're being timed."

"So you won't forget, will you?" Mom threw her marker down on the clipboard, then turned and faced the rest of the gang. "Ha!" she said. "This from a girl who forgets to brush her hair?"

Abby laughed nervously. Then Ronald and Philip joined in. I felt my face turn hot. I glared at Mom, then raced up the stairs and into my bedroom. I could hear Mom running after me. She knocked on the door, and when I didn't answer she came in silently and sat down on the bed.

"I'm sorry, Roxanne, I don't know what got into me," she said. "Can you ever forgive me?"

I kept my head turned down into my pillow and didn't move for the longest time. Then Mom reached over and started stroking my hair, like she used to when I was four and couldn't sleep.

"You were right. I got carried away with that assertiveness business."

"It's okay," I said, finally.

"No, it's not," Mom said. "It will never happen again."

Ronald's mother called later. I was already in bed but I couldn't sleep. I overheard Mom talking. Apparently, Ronald had a terrible case of anxiety. His mother was afraid that he'd be even more upset at the rehearsal on Wednesday. Then Abby's mom called. It seemed that Abby had broken into tears when she got home and confessed that she never thought the team would make it to the rehearsal, let alone all the way to the competition. Her mother said Abby was petrified by the prospect of appearing in front of the TV cameras again. Sometime after that, Philip's dad called. According to him, Philip was shaking so badly he couldn't hold a fork. His dad wondered if he would be able to press the buzzer.

I stayed awake for hours thinking about Claudia and Edgebrook Academy and their matching uniforms. Dad always says that knowing the rules is half the battle, but just looking like a team seemed like half the battle to me. If we looked fearless, like Edgebrook, we'd probably have a lot better chance of winning. I started to think about Trip and his friends and how they had looked on his thirteenth birthday. They all were wearing 3-D glasses and they let me try on a pair. The frames were white cardboard with a red cellophane lens on the right eye and a blue lens on the left. We looked like killer bees.

That's when it hit me. We should wear the 3-D glasses! They'd be better than any old uniform. They'd be an awesome disguise!

I snuck down to the kitchen and opened the middle drawer. The glasses were behind the birthday candles. I pulled them out and counted them.

Luckily, there were four.

I waited for Dad all Wednesday afternoon. I was practically frantic by the time he finally came home. It was four-thirty and Mom and Trip were already getting ready to leave for the rehearsal.

"Dad, it's about time," I cried, when he walked through the door. I expected to be mad at him, but he looked so tired I ran up and gave him a hug.

"I'm home," he called out to the rest of the family.

"Hi, Dad," Trip called back.

"Be with you in a second, dear," Mom yelled.

Dad winked at me, then he asked, "Well, Rox, are you ready for the big rehearsal?"

"I sure am," I said. The 3-D glasses were in my jacket. Dad slumped down on the couch and let out a long sigh. I sat down next to him and drummed my fingers on my knee. After a while, Dad pushed up his shirt sleeve and looked at his watch. It was already twenty minutes to five!

"Betsy! Trip! We'd better hurry. We don't want to be late," Dad called.

"Coming," Trip yelled.

"Be right with you," came Mom's muffled voice. I could hear her clinking hangers in the bedroom closet.

Trip and Dad and I waited in the car for Mom. It was four forty-nine by the time she jumped into the front seat. She rummaged around in her purse, pulled out a stick of gum, and popped it in her mouth. She was wearing her beige knit dress. Her face looked white and her lips trembled. Dad seemed shocked at her appearance. He looked worried as he turned around and smiled at Trip and me.

We were just turning down Elm Street when Mom said, "Bill, can you swing by the store? We need some milk."

Dad glanced at his watch and made a face.

"Well, honey, can't we do that later? We'll just get to the rehearsal on time as it is."

Mom ran her fingers through her hair, turned around quickly, and looked at Trip and me. She tried to smile, but her lips were drawn into a tight line.

"The thing is . . ." she said, clearing her throat. "I don't think I can go through with this."

"Betsy, you'll be fine." Dad reached across the seat and patted her hand. "Take a few deep breaths."

Trip nudged me. "I warned you," he whispered.

I sat real still and prayed that Mom wouldn't blow it, not tonight, not when we needed her most.

When we pulled into the parking lot at Edgebrook Academy, Dad let out a whistle.

"Will you look at the size of this parking lot! And when I think of how long it took us to raise the money for that little asphalt turnaround at Lazy Hills." Trip and I got out of the car but Mom stayed inside. She was sitting very still and staring straight ahead. Dad motioned us to go on without them.

Once inside, Abby, Ronald, Philip, and I were herded onto the stage in the new auditorium. Down below were about five hundred plush velvet seats. Floodlights lit up the front of the stage. The wooden floor was so shiny, I could see my reflection in it. I looked shabby and felt out of place in my old Burger Barn T-shirt. When I noticed that Abby, Ronald, and Philip were dressed in ragged T-shirts, too, I felt worse. We looked like "Creatures from the Murky Beyond."

The kids on the Edgebrook team were wearing matching polo shirts with tiny embroidered eagles on the collars. They looked like they had just stepped out of a Disney movie. Several of them poked each other when they saw us coming. One girl said, "Hey, didn't you take the wrong turn? The gym's down the hall." I expected Claudia to jump right in, but she didn't say a word. She sat stiffly behind a plaque that read TEAM CAPTAIN.

Miss High directed us to the long table facing the Edgebrook team. Instead of walking right over and taking our seats, we all seemed to freeze. When Abby turned around, I saw the blank look on her face—the same one she had during the "Around Town" interview.

I nudged Ronald and he started shuffling toward the table. I guess the stage lights hurt his eyes because he closed them. He looked just like Frankenstein when he bumped into the edge of the table and knocked the buzzers onto the floor. The players on the Edgebrook team were snickering. My knees were shaking, but somehow I managed to sit down and hang my jacket over the back of my chair.

Suzy Slooder made an announcement. "I'm afraid the 'Live at Five' crew had to cover a fire on the other side of Leesville, so we won't have a chance to rehearse with cameras."

Suddenly, Claudia tossed her head back, looked at us, and laughed. Then she poked the girl sitting next to her and mouthed, "Look, it's the losers from Lazy Hills." I tried to ignore her and concentrate on the rest of Suzy's speech.

"Parents," she said, "you are welcome to stay. In fact, I have found it helps to have the players get used to a live audience." Then Suzy turned to us. "Players, I will be asking a number of questions so you can get the feel of it. Just relax and have fun. We're not keeping score. Now, I'd like you to test your buzzers."

I glanced at Abby. Her hand was lifeless and resting on the table. It looked like something out of a wax museum. Her face was white and she stared straight ahead. Philip's hand was shaking so badly he missed the buzzer and hit my hand instead. The kids on the Edgebrook team were pressing their buzzers like crazy.

"We're dead!" Philip said.

I took a deep breath and pressed firmly on the red button. It made a short, loud buzzing sound. I looked for Mom, but she was nowhere in sight. Then Dad came over and gave us last-minute instructions.

"Roxanne, remember, as captain of the team it's up to you to make any final decisions," he said. "We're rooting for you!"

I took another deep breath. I tried to look at Abby and Ronald and Philip, but it was too depressing. I glanced over at Claudia, but the gleam in her eyes made me nervous. I probably would have been all right if I hadn't decided to look out at the audience. The seats were filling up with parents. I felt hot, then cold and queasy.

Suzy Slooder was talking. I could hear her voice but I couldn't make out the words. They sounded like they were coming from underwater. I leaned back in my chair and caught a glimpse of Mom and Dad. They were standing in the wings. Mom was gripping the curtain. Her knuckles were white and her face was pale. Dad gave me his thumbs-up sign.

I felt like I was drowning. It was almost time to begin. I took a deep breath and felt my ears pop.

"Don't forget, when you think you know the

answer, press your buzzer," Suzy said. "Shall we begin?"

She asked the first question. Claudia slammed her buzzer. The electronic timer started ticking loudly. It sounded like a giant clicker.

Throughout the first half, Claudia pressed the buzzer without hesitation. She seemed so sure of herself, she was a whiz! My head felt like it was filled with cotton instead of brains. When I did manage to press the buzzer, I forgot the answer.

We were taking a short break when I remembered the 3-D glasses. I passed them out. Reluctantly, we put them on. I must admit, we looked pretty ridiculous. Still, just wearing them made me feel better. I looked straight at Claudia and even though it was hard to see her clearly, I felt my heart rate slowing down to almost normal.

During the last half, I answered several questions correctly. So did Philip and Ronald.

"What famous baseball player hit 563 home runs, ranking him sixth in home-run history?"

Philip slammed down the buzzer and fired back, "Reggie Jackson!"

The second to the last question was about bacteria. I pressed the buzzer for Abby and kept my fingers crossed. She answered without a hitch. We were all tense, waiting for the last question.

"What is the capital of Florida?" asked Suzy.

I slammed my buzzer. But Claudia beat me by a

millisecond. Their team formed a huddle. I could see they were arguing.

"Orlando," said Claudia.

"Incorrect," said Suzy Slooder. "Lazy Hills, can you take it?"

We huddled. I thought about the Florida section in my *Little Student's Magic World* encyclopedia. All I could come up with was an image of a giant palm tree. I glanced up at the timer. We only had ten seconds left.

"Take it, Abby," I whispered.

"It begins with a T," Abby said.

"Is that your final answer?" asked Suzy.

"Yes," I said.

"I'm sorry. I can't accept that," said Suzy.

When it was all over, everybody got up from the table but me.

Suzy came over. It was hard to hear her because of all the cheering. She leaned down, pointed to my glasses, and said something.

"What?" I cried, cupping my ear.

"These," she said, lifting the glasses from my face. "The glasses have to go."

"Why?"

"Our viewing audience wants to see your bright, perky faces," she said.

I could see Mom on the other side of the stage, gathering up Abby, Ronald, and Philip.

She had them sit down at our table, then said, "I think we should reconsider going through with the game on Saturday."

Dad and Trip and Suzy came over and started to listen.

"What I mean is, I think it might be wiser if we went ahead and forfeited the game." Mom's voice was shaky.

"You mean quit?" I couldn't believe what Mom was saying. Trip had been right. I felt betrayed. I had to beat my fists against my legs to keep from crying. I pushed my chair back and stood up.

"You're a chicken!" I yelled at Mom. "You were so afraid of losing, you didn't even go to your own audition." My voice kept getting louder. "*You* may be afraid of losing, but we're not!"

Mom looked at me in horror, then slumped down in a chair. She looked like all the wind had been knocked out of her. I wanted to take back what I had said, but it was too late. Dad and Suzy were both shocked. I could feel tears streaming down my cheeks.

I raced off the stage and through the halls out into the parking lot. I ran past our car and kept on running. I wasn't even sure where I was going until I remembered the shortcut to McGiver Field. It was only five blocks if I cut through the cross-country track. The sun was setting as I reached the field.

I ran across the baseball diamond and collapsed,

sobbing, on the bottom bleacher. I buried my head in my hands and thought about what I had done. In three short weeks I had ruined everything. I had lost the championship game for our team and let Claudia get the better of me. I had embarrassed Mr. Duggins, almost lost Abby as my best friend, and betrayed Mom. There were things about myself I didn't like. I wished I could disappear.

In the distance, I heard a barn owl hooting. That made me feel even sadder. When I finally looked up, the sky had turned a clear dark blue. I stared at the stars for the longest time. The cool breeze made me shiver and I had to wrap my arms around myself to keep warm.

I was just getting up to leave, when I saw Dad pull up in the car.

He walked across the field toward me, carrying the car blanket.

"I thought I might find you here," he said softly. When he sat down beside me, the bleacher creaked. He wrapped the blanket around my shoulders.

"Leave me alone," I said, wriggling away from the blanket.

"I think we ought to have a little Bookman powwow," he said.

"Don't talk to me, then, because I'm not a Bookman. Bookmans are winners, remember. I'm a loser."

"I deserved that," he said. "On the drive over, I

thought a lot about you and how I put pressure on you to win. I didn't mean to. It's just that I'm so proud of our little family that sometimes I go overboard. I'm especially proud of you, Roxanne."

"Proud of me?"

"Absolutely. I'm proud of you for picking yourself up after that ball game, and taking on a new challenge."

"Really?"

"Really! Why just last month I almost backed out of bidding for the bridge contract. I just didn't think my company had a chance. But then I thought about you and Trip and your mom, and I knew I had to try."

I moved closer to Dad.

We sat there for a while, then I said, "I shouldn't have said those things tonight. I'm sorry."

"And I shouldn't have said all that stuff about winning," he said. "I guess we've both learned something, right?"

"Right."

He pulled me up and smiled. With his arm around my shoulder, we walked back to the car.

In the morning, my conscience was still bothering me. I felt sad and lonely. And the sound of rain beating against my window didn't help. I crept down the stairs. I heard Dad humming. He was in the kitchen making breakfast, so I went on back to Mom and Dad's bedroom. I knocked on the door.

"Yes?" Mom answered.

I peered into the room.

"Mom, I'm sorry about last night," I said.

She patted a spot on the bed and motioned me to come sit down. I hurried over and hugged her, then sank down on the bed next to her. I didn't know what to say, so I just sat there.

Mom broke the silence. "Last night, I was convinced that we should forfeit. After all, your dad doesn't really have time to coach and I haven't done a very good job of handling the pressure. Then your dad and I talked it over and I realized that I would just be running away again. I guess what I'm trying to say is, I'm going to stay on and fight. And I know just the person to help me."

I did a lot of thinking on the way to school. Despite Mom's brave words, I just knew I couldn't make her go through coaching again. I had gotten us into this mess and it was my job to get us out. I made up my mind to call Miss High after lunch and officially forfeit the game.

All morning, I dreaded making the call.

Abby, Ronald, and Philip met me at our table in the lunchroom. I expected them to look happy and relieved. After all, I was sure they agreed with Mom that we should forfeit the game. It was what they'd been hoping for all along. Instead, they looked upset.

"You have to talk your mom into letting us stay in the contest," Ronald said.

Abby and Philip nodded their heads in agreement.

"Why?" I asked. "I thought you wanted to quit."

"That was before the glasses, silly," Abby explained. She looked at the others like I was crazy or something.

"Yeah, that was before we knew we could win," Ronald said.

I had to tell them. "About the glasses . . . Suzy Slooder told me we can't use them."

"You're kidding," said Philip.

"I've decided to call Miss High and forfeit the game," I said, looking down. When I looked up again, they were hunched over, staring at a spot in the center of the table. I stared, too. We must have been zapped by aliens.

Then something happened to cheer us up. Mr. Duggins walked right over to our table, pulled out a chair, sat down, and said, "I've just had a long talk with your mother, Roxanne. We're going to tackle our problems head on."

"Oh," I said. I didn't know what else to say. I didn't know what he was talking about.

"Bookman, don't you get it?" he said. "Your mom and I are going to coach the team!"

"Wonderful," said Ronald, his face lighting up.

"Terrific," agreed Philip.

"Are you sure it's a good idea?" I asked.

"What's the matter with you, Roxanne? Of course it's a good idea," said Abby. "Mr. Duggins, can we practice today?"

"The team will resume practice tomorrow," he declared. "Right now, I'm in the mood for Twenty Questions."

He leaned back in his chair and folded his hands across his stomach. "Gee, I wonder if I'm a famous person, place, or thing," he teased. "Okay, gang, I'm ready."

"Are you a person?" Ronald asked.

"Yes."

"Living?"

"Nope."

"Are you a fictional character?" asked Philip.

"Yes."

"Are you in the entertainment industry?" I asked.

"He said fictional, Roxanne," Philip said.

"Well, in a way I am in the entertainment industry," he said. "But not the way you think."

"You aren't in politics, are you?" Abby asked.

"No."

By the time we reached question twenty, we were still stumped.

"Ah-ha!" he cried. "I'm Rip Van Winkle!"

"Who's Rip Van Winkle?" I asked.

"It's in the library, Bookman. Check it out. You'll love it. It's fantastic! Hilarious! Rip-roaring fun!"

On Friday, our team met in the classroom after the last bell. Mr. Duggins was dressed in normal clothes again. He was sitting calmly on the edge of his desk, when Mom rushed in from work. She was carrying a briefcase and a collapsible cardboard file. She handed them to Mr. Duggins.

"I went ahead and put the questions into categories under each subject heading. That way, we can work systematically through each section," she said, pulling up a chair.

"Great!" he boomed. He flipped through the file. "Since we talked, I've had a few ideas of my own."

"I'd love to hear them," said Mom.

"Okay, let's toss these up and see how they fly," he said.

He hopped down from his desk, turned to the

blackboard and started scribbling little stick people, then connecting them with arrows.

"Picture this as our team," he said, pointing to the little stick figures. "These arrows indicate the various plays that each teammate can run. Get it?"

I think it's safe to say that none of us knew what he was talking about.

"Mr. Duggins, it's not like baseball," I said. "We just sit there and answer the questions." I was beginning to get that old sinking feeling.

"Ah-ha!" he cried. "That's the problem. It *is* a series of plays. Look," he continued. "You have to lean toward the buzzer. Correct?"

"Correct," we said, puzzled.

"And press the buzzer. Correct?"

"Correct," we answered, more loudly. I heard Mom's voice chime in.

"And huddle."

"Correct!" We were yelling now.

"And watch the timer."

"Correct!" we shouted.

"And answer into the microphone."

"Correct!" We were jumping up and down.

"That's what I call a series of plays," he said, sitting back down on the desk.

"What a great game plan!" cried Mom.

"Then what are we waiting for?" yelled Mr. Duggins. "Let's go to Edgebrook and work on our strategy."

Edgebrook Academy was deserted when we arrived. All the kids had gone home. The "Live at Five" news crew was in the auditorium setting up video monitors and checking the microphones. We watched for a few minutes and then got down to the business of learning how to beat Edgebrook Academy.

Mr. Duggins didn't make us nervous like Mom had. He didn't even set the timer.

"Forget it," he said. "Just forget it's here."

"What about the TV cameras?" Abby asked.

"Forget 'em," said Mr. Duggins. "Or better yet, pretend they're bugs from Mars."

Abby started laughing. She seemed much more comfortable. While we worked on our plays, Mom talked with the TV crew. I could see that she was giving them pointers about positioning the cameras.

"What about Claudia?" I asked. "Just thinking about her makes me shudder!"

Abby and Ronald and Philip nodded their heads in agreement.

"An Earthling!" he said, waving his hand. "A mere mortal! Think of yourselves as superior beings from another planet."

"What about the audience?" Ronald asked.

"That's the best part," said Mr. Duggins. "Imagine they are your alien fan club with invisible antennae on their heads."

I looked out over the empty auditorium and imagined it filling up with alien creatures. This was going to be fun!

We spent an hour practicing our plays. We leaned, pressed, huddled, and answered. By the end of the hour, we were like robots. We moved with precision. We didn't even notice the TV crew. We were more than four kids from Lazy Hills. We were a team. And we wanted to succeed. I know it sounds silly, but I don't think anything or anyone could have scared us, not even Claudia Slooder.

I expected to wake up feeling a little nervous on Saturday. Instead, I was whistling as I joined Mom and Dad at the breakfast table.

"Trip went on ahead to football practice," Mom told me calmly. "But he said to wish you luck." As she poured my glass of orange juice, I realized how pretty she looked in her bright purple blouse. Dad was gulping his coffee. It was funny; now he was more nervous than Mom.

By nine o'clock the whole gang was in the kitchen, except for Mr. Duggins. I wasn't worried until Dad started pacing the kitchen floor. He opened the back door and looked searchingly up and down the street.

"Where is he?" Dad moaned.

"Bill, maybe you should have a seat," Mom said in that tone of voice she gets when she wants him to calm down.

At nine-fifteen, Mr. Duggins pulled into the drive-way. He rushed into the kitchen, carrying the

Hornets' equipment box. I though he had flipped out for sure.

"Bookman!" he cried. "Come over here." He leaned over the box and started tossing out gloves and baseballs. "Here they are. They just arrived." He pulled out a stack of new red jerseys and matching caps. "I know it's not fancy, but it's better than nothing."

I thought I would feel silly wearing a cap that had a picture of a smiling hornet on the front. But I didn't.

When we walked onto the stage at Edgebrook Academy, the Eagles were already seated. They were wearing blue blazers with little gold eagles on the pockets. Surprisingly, Claudia and the other kids on the team didn't make their usual comments about Lazy Hills. I guess since Miss High was there, they were on their best behavior.

Miss High walked over and greeted us.

"Good morning, Lazy Hills," she said, smiling. "I want to wish each of you the best of luck today." She went down the row, shaking our hands.

Suzy Slooder breathed into the microphone. "Testing One! Two! Three!" Her voice echoed across the auditorium.

The audience was arriving.

"Remember, think of them as Martians with antennae on their heads," I told the rest of the team. Abby started giggling.

Mom was standing over by Suzy and the "Live at Five" crew. Suzy was sorting out giant cue cards.

And the cameraman was wheeling a huge camera around in front of the tables. I poked Abby and she mouthed, "What a hunk!"

Then I heard Mom.

"Excuse me," she said, clearing her throat. Suzy and the rest of the crew stopped what they were doing to listen.

"Wouldn't it be better, I mean, wouldn't it make a stronger visual statement, if the teams' tables were closer together?"

"Yes, I see your point," said Suzy thoughtfully. "That's a wonderful idea, Betsy." We got up while the crew pushed the tables closer together; then we sat back down again. I glanced over at Claudia. She was pale and had a blank look on her face. I wondered what was wrong with her.

One of the crew members held up a giant cue card that read APPLAUSE. Everyone started clapping. Then Suzy Slooder sort of sprinted up to the podium. She was smiling broadly. She introduced the teams, starting with the captains. Claudia didn't budge when her name was mentioned. I tried to smile into the camera, but I felt dizzy. I think I was looking cross-eyed.

"Let's begin!" cried Suzy.

"What common butterfly makes a yearly migration?"

I pressed the buzzer first. Edgebrook didn't even try this one.

The electronic timer started ticking. We huddled.

"Monarch!" I shouted into the microphone.

"Correct," Suzy shouted.

The applause was deafening. I could see Mr. Duggins standing in the wings. He tipped his cap and smiled.

On the second question, our team was the first to buzz. I gave it to Abby.

"What common edible fungus is used in tossed salads?"

"Mushrooms," she answered confidently.

Suzy asked another question. "When Reggie Jackson played for the New York Yankees, he was given a nickname. What was it?"

Philip slammed the buzzer and jumped up. "Mr. October!" he shouted.

"Mr. October is correct."

Suzy went on to the next question. "Define adjective."

I leaned, pressed, and gave it to Philip.

"It's something that says something about something else," he said.

Suzy looked down at her answer sheet, then glanced over at the hidden panel of judges.

"I'm sorry, I can't accept that," she said. "Edgebrook, can you take it?"

There was silence from the Edgebrook team. They didn't even attempt to answer the question. They were all looking at Claudia. Her chin was quivering and she looked like she was going to cry. I tried not to look at her. After all, we were winning and that was the important thing.

For the next fifteen questions, we leaned, pressed, huddled, and answered. It should have been exciting but really, and this is the weird part, it began to be boring. Also, it was embarrassing pushing the buzzers and answering when no one from the Edgebrook team was even trying. By the end of the first half, the score was Lazy Hills 18, Edgebrook 0.

We were winning. But as we walked down to the media center for our fifteen-minute break, I realized that none of us seemed too thrilled. The kids from the Edgebrook team were already there. We all sat on the swivel chairs and stared at each other, except for Claudia. She walked to the other side of the room, sat down, and started crying.

I looked at Abby. I guess we both felt kind of bad for her. Abby walked over to see if she could help and I followed.

"Come on, Claudia, what's wrong?" I said.

She kept sobbing.

"Is it the timer?" asked Abby.

Claudia shook her head no. I tried to think. During the rehearsal there had been a timer, and buzzers, and even an audience. Then I remembered. The "Live at Five" news crew had been covering a fire.

"The cameras!" I cried.

Claudia nodded yes between sobs.

"Forget 'em!" Abby said.

Claudia looked so pathetic, I tried to make a joke of it. "Better yet, pretend they're big bugs from Mars."

Claudia looked up. Her eyes were glistening with tears. Then she smiled. "Thanks," she said. "You're really nice to say that after all I've done to you. Everyone's going to hate me after today. We're going to lose and it's all my fault."

I don't know why, but I said, "You just need to be more sure of yourself, like you are on the baseball field."

"Yeah, you need to be assertive," Abby said.

"You're right," Claudia said.

Suddenly everyone on our team was talking and laughing with everyone on their team. Ronald and Philip went over the plays with them. They leaned, pressed, huddled, and answered. We were having such a great time, we didn't even notice Miss High when she came to get us for the second half.

"I think we can beat you!" Claudia said.

"We'll see about that," I called back. Secretly, I was sure we would win. I didn't see how they could catch up to us. After all, we had an eighteen-point lead. Then something Suzy said made me worry.

She sprinted to the podium. "Welcome back to 'Brain Teaser.' Before we begin, I'd like to remind the team captains that the scoring changes in the second half. Each answer is now worth two points."

"Yikes!" I said to Abby. "Edgebrook really can catch us!"

The rest of the contest went by in a blur. Claudia and the kids from Edgebrook seemed to have the buzzers built into their fingertips. The audience was going wild. By the fourth quarter, we'd only answered three questions to their ten. The score was 24 to 20, our favor. We were neck and neck.

"What's a dozen dozen called?" Suzy asked quickly.

Abby and Claudia slammed their buzzers at almost the same moment.

"Edgebrook!" said Suzy.

They didn't huddle. They had it. "A gross."

"Correct."

There was more applause. It was Lazy Hills 24, Edgebrook 22.

"There are two minutes left to play. Here's our next question," said Suzy. "What is a botanist?"

Ronald and Claudia leaned and pressed their buzzers.

"Lazy Hills!" said Suzy.

We huddled. None of us knew the answer, so I gave it to Ronald.

"A person who buys things," he said, finally.

There was a ripple of laughter from the audience.

"Incorrect," said Suzy. "Edgebrook, can you take it?"

"One who studies plants," said Claudia.

"That is correct."

There were screams from the Edgebrook section. The score was tied, 24 to 24.

"We'll be back with our final question following this commercial break," said Suzy. While she flipped through her stack of questions, I looked out at the audience. Some of the kids from class were cheering wildly. I expected to see Dad carrying Mom out of the place, but they were sitting quietly in the second row. Mom was smiling. Then Mr. Duggins came over and gave us some last-minute pointers.

"Take your time," he said. "And remember, you're a team. If you're not sure of the answer, talk it over."

A red light started blinking on and off at the podium and Mr. Duggins hurried from the stage. I took a deep breath and sat up straight in my chair. I had my hand poised over the buzzer when I heard Claudia whisper my name.

"Hey, Roxanne, may the best team win," she said with a self-assured grin on her face.

"Don't worry, we will," I said, grinning back at her. Then I leaned over toward Abby, Philip, and Ronald. "Okay, you guys, let's go for it!"

Suzy rushed back into position. She raised her arms to the deafening applause. "Isn't this exciting?" she cried. There were cheers and whistles. She brought her arms down and signaled for the audience to settle down. "As you all know, we have a tie situation." There was another short burst of cheering from the audience. "The team that answers the next question correctly will be the new 'Brain Teaser' champions. Audience, we ask that you remain quiet, please! Captains, are your teams ready?"

Claudia and I both nodded our heads.

"Let's begin," Suzy said. "The famous words 'Four score and seven years ago' were uttered by President Abraham Lincoln. Name the speech, please."

I slammed my hand down on the buzzer.

"Lazy Hills!" Suzy said.

"I'm pretty sure I know this one," I whispered to the rest of the team. Then I remembered what Mr. Duggins had said about teamwork. I called a huddle. "I think it's the Gettysburg Treaty."

"No, it's not treaty," said Philip.

"It's something like diary or directory," said Abby. She closed her eyes and snapped her fingers. "You know, that little book where you keep the names of friends and their street numbers . . ."

I glanced up at the timer. We only had five seconds to answer.

"You mean an address book," whispered Ronald.

"Address, that's it! Take it, Ronald," I cried. Ronald was on his feet.

"The Gettysburg Address," he shouted.

"That is absolutely, positively, correct," said Suzy. "Congratulations! Ladies and gentlemen, our new champions, Lazy Hills Elementary School!"

The audience went wild. Abby, Philip, Ronald, and I were jumping up and down, screaming. "We did it! We won!"

After the game, our team piled into Mr. Duggins's convertible and headed for the Burger Barn. Mom and Dad followed us in the station wagon.

By the time we got there, it was packed. Even Trip's football team was there.

"Here, Joe, let me help," Trip said when he saw us come in. He dashed around the counter and tied a cook's apron around his waist.

Since most of the booths were filled, we had to sit on the stools at the counter. Mr. Duggins put our trophy up on the counter for everyone to see. I sat next to the little glass jukebox. Philip was between my parents, but he didn't seem to mind.

"Joe!" yelled Mr. Duggins. "How about cheeseburgers and chocolate malts all around? Is that all right with you?" He turned to Mom and Dad.

I thought Dad would want to order something weird, but he surprised me.

"Sure," he said. "Could you load mine with chili, Joe?"

"Yes, extra onions on mine, if you don't mind," said Mom.

While we were waiting for our food, Miss High and the Edgebrook team came in.

"Joe, another round of cheeseburgers and chocolate malts, this time for our friends from Edgebrook Academy. It's on me," boomed Mr. Duggins. Everyone on the Edgebrook team started to cheer. Then they walked over and started congratulating us.

"I guess the best team won," Claudia said. She held out her hand to me.

"Thanks, Claudia," I said, shaking her hand. "But you were pretty awesome toward the end."

"That's true," she said. "The next time we play, we're going to smash you guys."

"Oh, really," I said.

"Yeah, really!"

Then we both started laughing. Ronald and Philip hopped down from their stools and started talking to some of the Edgebrook kids.

"Claudia, you can sit here if you want," I said, pointing to the stool next to mine.

"Thanks," she said.

Then Claudia and Abby and I flipped through the jukebox selections, which were really corny and about a zillion years old. When Joe brought out a platter of cheeseburgers, we dove right in.

"I'd almost forgotten how great an authentic Burger Barn cheeseburger could be," Mom said, wiping catsup from the corners of her mouth.

"Remember when we used to have them after a dance?" asked Dad. He had a goofy smile on his face.

I bit into my cheeseburger. It was hot and juicy and delicious. Abby was making happy slurping sounds with her straw when Mr. Duggins began telling another *Mad Men from Mars* story. It seems Mom and Dad had read the stories, too, because they jumped right in whenever Mr. Duggins left something out.

Then Mom and Dad did something that made me want to disappear. They picked three of the worst songs on the jukebox and started dancing this weird dance.

"It's called the Mashed Potato," Mom yelled over to me. They were picking each leg up and shaking it. I can't really describe it except to say they looked like giant chickens. I was sure my nightmare was coming true, until I noticed that Mr. Duggins and Miss High had joined them.

"Come on, don't be party poopers," hollered Mr. Duggins.

Pretty soon we were all dancing, even Trip.

CATHY WARREN is also the author of *Saturday Belongs to Sara,* illustrated by DyAnne DiSalvo-Ryan, which ALA *Booklist* calls "as sweet as a kiss," adding that "Sara's emotions are carefully captured, and children will appreciate the dignity given to her feelings."

Cathy Warren lives with her family in Davidson, North Carolina. *Roxanne Bookman: Live at Five!* is her first novel.